It's Not A Secret

Max Turner

ISBN:1975883985
ISBN-13: 978-1975883980

AUTHOR'S NOTE

I originally wrote this as fan fiction, so there is some assumed knowledge of the characters. I decided to print it because I feel like there is a bit of a lack of gay romance featuring a trans character and would love to see more of it myself from any source.

This is hopefully all the background you will need for the characters and story -
Adam: Known to be promiscuous, trans gay man. Once smart, sassy and rude his confidence is low at the beginning of the story. Throughout this story he is transitioning and dealing with the mental, emotional and physical strains of doing so. Works in journalism, with a lot of assholes.
Elias: Rude, disagreeable grump, who combats his low self-confidence by putting on extreme and self-serving bravado. He has a medical condition that causes him to have inappropriate erections that he has to deal with (I know it sounds cracky, but actually sensitively handled). He's low on friends and often not likeable. Works as a translator of manuscripts for a publisher.

Background characters... I borrowed from a TV show and gave them a little twist as they just felt right in the context of this story.

WARNINGS

This story includes a Trans main character. There are misunderstandings, confusion, ignorant behaviour, misgendering, transphobic behaviour/language, binding, packing, gender dysphoria, top surgery, lower surgery, some angst, friends to lovers, slow burn romance, happy ending. Explicit sex scenes: fingering (vaginal and anal), penetration (vaginal and anal), butt plugs, blow jobs, pegging.

CONTENTS

ACKNOWLEDGMENTS

To everyone in the fandom who supported this story, gave beautiful feedback and shared with me their own experiences. I can't tell you what the massively positive reception of this story has meant to me.

1

Elias licked his lips as he watched the girl across the bar. He had been watching her for a while - her slender but firm shape, her dark curls not quite shoulder length. He was mesmerised, not least by the way she threw her head back when she laughed at whatever the guy she was with was saying. The green scarf she was wearing made it difficult to get an exact view of her from where he sat only able to see her back and partial side view - but it was enjoyable nonetheless.

Elias ran through scenarios in his head of dating such a woman. Maybe that specific woman if she could be wrested from the man that accompanied her. He shifted in his chair slightly, feeling the familiar stirring below, but thankfully nothing that would require him to leave at this stage. At least that allowed him to continue observing as he sipped at his beer where he sat alone in the Soho bar on a quiet Sunday afternoon.

That man with her clearly not did not deserve such an attentive and beautiful date. And that was all the more confirmed when the man stood abruptly and began to talk aggressively to the beauty. Elias wasn't close enough to hear what was being said but the gestures and the man's expression concerned him. Elias looked around and saw a barman on his way over to the commotion, but other patrons who were closer did nothing, keeping their heads down and ignoring the situation.

Elias would have, of course, never done such a thing! Gabriel was always telling him that he did not do all he said he would do, that he made things up and exaggerated. As if Gabriel knew anything! Elias huffed inwardly. He couldn't help it if his brother didn't witness him at such things and especially realise his prowess with beautiful women. The thought of their

1

rather annoying argument the night before, exactly about this, drove Elias to his feet and across the room.

The man was indeed swearing and looked angry, the woman snapping back - clearly upset.

"You should not talk that way to a lady!" Elias admonished him once he was beside the woman.

They both stopped shouting and the man looked at him, indignation was chased off his face by astonishment and then the man laughed. A cruel and angry laugh that made Elias mad. He didn't like being laughed at and had done nothing that should have invited this.

"Piss off!" The man finally said as his laughter subsided.

"Don't…" the woman started, her voice was melodic, and Elias was glad to have been able to hear it.

"Don't talk to me, freak!" The man was shouting at the woman again.

She replied "*I'm* the freak? You're the one asking strangers to be in your private fucking video collection!" Her words were full of rage and she was using very unladylike language that might have put Elias off if he hadn't seen that the situation made it completely understandable.

The barman was suddenly alongside them and asking everyone to leave.

"I'm not leaving, I have done nothing!" Elias looked back to his lone table with half of his drink sitting untouched, a silly waste.

"Just keep out of this." The man said angrily and he went to grab the woman's arm and pull her off her chair. Elias saw red at that as she squealed at his tight grasp. He swung a punch.

And then it was a mess.

Fists were flying and he wasn't sure who was who. The barman was shouting now that he was going to call the police as Elias was pushed into one of the empty bar stools and took a stumble. Then he felt his arm being tugged and he was outside, being pulled along the London street just fresh from rain. He was pulled around a corner just as he heard the sirens of a police car pull up behind them.

The hand that had been pulling him let go and they stopped, both panting as he looked up into a glorious smile that made his heart sing in his chest.

"Hey. Thanks. You were just trying to help, I didn't want you to get into trouble for my sake."

Elias focused and took in the unobstructed view of the woman that he had saved and who had saved him in return. Only… it wasn't a woman. Not quite.

She was wearing almost all black except a green scarf that obscured her chest, where his eyes had been drawn for a confirmation. Elias was sure she was a woman but… there was something not feminine about her that he couldn't quite put his finger on. He noticed then that her smile had vanished, her face had fallen and Elias realised he was scrutinising her.

"Well. Thanks again." She said and turned to walk away, deflated. It made Elias sad to know he had caused that and he grabbed her hand. Gabriel had told him before about looking at women in such a way, he cursed himself, and then his brother for being right - as unusual as that was.

"I'm sorry. Are you ok? Were you hurt?" He asked.

She spun and pulled her hand away, looking at first shocked and angry that he had touched her and Elias scolded himself again, but then she seemed to soften and replied - "Just my feelings. As usual. Just when you think the world is a better place…" her words were full of a biting humour and she trailed off into a little smile. "I'm Adam, what's-"

"I should walk you home, miss." Elias interrupted her, nodding and suddenly unsure what to do in such a situation. He decided on chivalry and barely taking in anything she said as he talked over the lady "It might not be safe for ladies at night."

The woman's face fell in a way he had never seen before. Disappointment, sadness, and all directed at him. How rude! Surely she would know that some men were not as honourable as he was.

"I'm fine." Her voice was cold as she backed away from him and turned. This time when she walked away and Elias didn't stop her.

*

Oh fuck.

Adam looked over and saw that the person standing next to him at the bar was the moustached foreigner that had stepped in on that awful blind date he'd had a few months earlier in another local pub. *One* of the dates anyway, before he finally gave up on dating altogether. And now this guy was here to rake up a shitty memory! He really didn't want to have to deal with mis-gendering tonight, his day had already been bad enough.

He'd thought being a journalist had been difficult as a woman, but that felt like a cake walk some days since he had started to medically transition. At least he was passing more now, the months of testosterone finally paying off. It just sucked that they also made him horny as fuck but getting laid wasn't always that easy. Like the blind date that he'd been on when he had met the guy next to him now. They were both clear that it was going to be a hook up, but the guy had got shitty when Adam had said no to the guy filming it. Another fucking fetishist. Which to be honest he didn't always turn away if he was that horny, but he wasn't hard up enough to let the asshole film it for his celluloid wank bank.

He'd been surprised and grateful when the European guy had stepped in - all blustering indignation topped with curly hair and an interesting face. Things had been weird and tense and aggressive. And every fucking person in there had put their head down and ignored the tranny being shouted at for not wanting to star in the asshole's sex tape. Adam sighed at the memory. How great it had been to have someone give a shit. But when the guy misgendered him even once they were out of the pub and Adam hoped he could clearly see him, it hurt. It always hurt.

It was getting less and less. Especially with new people he met that only knew him as Adam, but family, older friends and especially colleagues still got it wrong. Each time was like a little stab of hurt and doubt and sorrow.

He'd come out for a quiet drink with his two closest friends, he really didn't want to deal with any shit. He ducked his head as his order arrived and he grabbed the two pints and wine glass and re-joined his friends sitting near the back of the bar - breathing a sigh of relief when he sat.

"You ok?" Bev asked with her usual concern that bordered on overprotective.

"Yeah… just. That guy at the bar." He paused and let Bev and Bedelia look over his shoulder at the man. Bev grinned and Bedelia cocked a judgemental eyebrow - the man was wearing something his grandpa might, so Adam got her look. Unruly hair, porno moustache, on top of a pale polo shirt and spots jacket. It might as well still be 1992. "He was the one that helped me out when that Dave asshole got fucking weird."

Both women's brows shot up in acknowledgment, which on Bev then turned to a scowl.

"I still owe Jimmy a slap for setting you up with that jerk." Bev interjected with a mumbled threat.

Adam rolled his eyes. "Don't blame Jimmy. He didn't know the guy was a creep. Anyway, that isn't the point. I… I'd only been on T a couple of months. He thought I was a woman, it… I dunno, I just kinda feel weird about it." Even as he said it he felt waves of dysphoria rising in him, always so conscious of what he was or wasn't - at least in other people's eyes.

Bedelia grabbed for his hand and squeezed it. "We can go somewhere else?"

"No, no. It's fine. Dammit, I just… I hate feeling like this. I need to… It's ok. He probably doesn't even remember me. Won't recognise me." Adam smiled at the girls and then looked over his shoulder just as the guy looked up, his eyes finding Adam's as he lowered his glass and left beer foam in his moustache - which Adam might have found funny under other circumstances.

There was a flash of something there - maybe recognition. Adam looked quickly away and felt like curling into a ball. But he couldn't. He always knew this wasn't going to be easy, but some days were harder than he had the energy for.

Bev changed the subject then - more hilarious horror stories from the medical lab she worked in that had them all laughing. By rights it was really inappropriate to do so and they should have been disgusted but Bev did know how to tell an amusing tale. Adam started to relax again and after a while the pub got busy and Adam didn't see the European guy in the crowd. He didn't see him again until he went to the men's bathroom an hour later.

Adam tucked his STP back into his pants and left the cubicle, heading straight to the sink and turning the faucet before he even registered that the man washing his hands next to him was that European guy.

Adam clenched his jaw and washed his hands quickly, though not without noticing the guy stealing glances at him in the mirror - to the point where he seemed to have washed his hands several times whilst watching Adam. Finally Adam, pulling out some paper towels and, drying his hands, looked at the man's reflection and snapped -

"What?!"

The man seemed startled by the confrontation and then started grabbing at the paper towels - taking wads from the dispenser before finally starting to dry his hands.

"That's very rude!" The man responded, looking somewhere between aghast and annoyed.

Adam blinked. "You've been staring at me since I got to the sink. You don't think *that's* rude?" He was trying to stay calm despite wavering somewhere between anxious panic and rage.

"I was merely trying to place you. You seem familiar and I thought if we knew each other somehow, I should say hello as that would be polite."

Adam wasn't sure how to respond to that for a moment, feeling as though he had been chastised.

"We don't know each other." He finally huffed and started towards the door.

"Wait." The man said, stepping after him.

Adam turned in a way that mimicked that night in the alley. And that seemed to trigger it - the memory and realisation. The man's eyes went wide with confusion and curiosity. And then his eyes went to Adam's chest - bound though not completely passable as masculine, but enough to go unnoticed by those who didn't know or suspect. Those who didn't look too hard. Then the man's eyes went to his crotch and he frowned at the bulge there.

Adam felt heat flush up his neck - a mixture of embarrassment and anger. He felt exposed and vulnerable. He wanted to wrap his arms around his chest, cursing that he had taken his scarf off earlier and left it back in the bar. He was such an idiot, he shouldn't have taken it off! And yet in reality he knew it would have made little real difference to the situation beyond providing the comfort of feeling somewhat more hidden.

"What *is* your problem?" Adam finally snapped, unable to help the outburst though he knew he should just turn and walk out. He'd had friends in situations like this before and though he'd been lucky so far, he wasn't stupid. Being trans could be dangerous even in as open and accepting a place as this trendy bar in London's Soho.

The man looked taken aback. "No need to be rude."

Adam's eyes went wide with startled indignation. "Says the guy eyeing up my crotch!"

The man blustered for a moment, gesticulating and mumbling foreign words before finally responding in English - "It is very unladylike to dress this way and sneak into men's bathrooms! If you had been here a moment earlier I would have been stood at the urinal and you would have seen my penis! Very unladylike!"

Adam wondered if the horror showed on his face. He was caught somewhere between deep anger and a terrified mortification that gripped him and shook him from within. It played on all the worst fears and feelings of dysphoria and being in limbo and not being accepted. He wanted to run, wanted to turn and run out and go home and cry. But he didn't want this asshole and everyone like him to win. The ignorant, arrogant son of a bitch.

"You ignorant fucking asshole." Adam spat.

This time the foreigner looked on with indignation and seemed to be grasping for words before finding the completely wrong ones - "You are so very rude!" he jabbed a finger at Adam in a way that Adam had to assume was a physical threat. And that was all it took for self-preservation to take over and Adam to ball his fist and swing, catching the guy's deceptively solid jaw and throwing them both off centre. He regained his position quickly and Adam steeled himself for a fight, suddenly aware of how stupid he was being and the very real consequences of his actions. But… the man didn't strike back.

Instead he rubbed his jaw, tears welling in his eyes. "You hit me." The words were all but sobbed out and Adam felt a mixture of concern and confusion. He'd never made anyone cry like this before, it left him with a rotten feeling deep inside. Enough even to get him past some of his earlier feelings of discomfort and dysphoria.

"I… I shouldn't have. I'm sorry." He moved forward to offer help but the bigger man shied back from him. It felt like a punch to Adam's gut. "God, I'm so sorry. I've never… I didn't mean to… I just thought. I thought you were going to… damn, I'm so sorry."

The man looked up at him through weepy eyes, and he was clearly struggling to hold back tears. "I don't like being hit."

Adam felt guilt tear through him, more anger followed in its wake. "Well, ok, that was wrong of me. But I don't like to be misgendered and talked to like that!"

The man looked at him completely bewildered. "I don't understand what you're talking about. Misgenerated? I don't understand." He seemed confused and close to tears which made Adam freak out slightly. What the fuck was this? Was he really feeling bad for this guy?

Urgh.

"I'm sorry." He said again and reached a hand out to pat the guy's shoulder but he shrugged it off and ran from the room. Adam went after him but lost sight of him as he left the bar and headed out into the early evening.

He returned to their table and slumped into his chair grabbing up his scarf and wrap it around his neck before letting his head sink into his hands. "I need more to drink."

Bev went to the bar without stopping to ask questions.

*

Elias's eyes were sore from the tears he held back and his cheeks damp from those he'd been unable to, as he let himself into his small and dingy bedsit. It was all he could afford when he first moved to London, and now he had a job and was settled he just hadn't bothered doing anything about it. He was suddenly, and most illogically regretting that - looking around and considering that this would not be a nice place to bring a date home.

Such an odd thought. But then his mind was a little off kilter from his evening's experience.

The attractive and feisty lady he had helped some months ago, that he had even thought about running into again... may have even imagined her smile when taking care of the little problem he had... was a man? That couldn't be right. She looked like she had perhaps very small breasts - almost flat-chested. And her face was so beautiful, but... there was the bulge in her pants and she was using the men's room. Was there a slight stubble too? It was a little difficult to tell in the dimly lit toilets. But certainly there was something different enough that he didn't recognise her at first - her face had somehow changed. Become more masculine... but no less beautiful. Same lips that more than once Elias had thought about kissing.

So silly. He wasn't a teenager and shouldn't be mooning over women he met in bars. But there had been something about her. *Him?*

He shook his head. Confused by the woman, her words, her location, her bulge... her being a man? She had been so upset that he had almost felt bad, but she was so rude and then she struck him and now everything was sore and confusing and he wanted to just go to bed. But his cock was already starting to ache and he hated his condition more than anything in that moment. Because all he could see was her lovely face and now that picture was wrong, she wasn't real. Maybe he had imagined her?

He pressed down on his cock as he made his way to the bathroom, determined to push her from his thoughts. And yet, that beautiful, possibly stubbled face flashed in his mind as he came in his fist.

2

Adam took in a breath and let it out slowly, shaking a little as he looked in the mirror. It wasn't like it was the first time he had seen his chest since his top surgery, but he *had* been avoiding it the last couple of months. When the bandages had been removed the scarring had been so red and angry that he cried. He'd known to expect it, but the reality of it not being finally 100% perfect, had been a blow. He knew it was ridiculous. And he knew that he had healed just fine, but even so his chest remained a hurdle for him to overcome.

He tried not to dwell on it but continued to wear layer upon layer through the winter and well into spring even after it healed and even now that he didn't need to. Maybe it was habit from so many years binding, or maybe it was that niggling anxiety he had that he'd still feel dysphoric without those layers for comfort. Either way, the weather was getting too hot and he just had to start to deal with it.

He looked down at the vest in his hand, a top he had bought years ago when he had assumed he would be wearing that sort of thing as soon as surgery was healed. When he assumed it would magically give him the confidence to do so.

He was saved from making the decision or looking back to the mirror, by his phone beeping. The message was from Bev telling him to get his ass in gear or she would make him be designated driver instead. He smiled. She always knew the right way to motivate him.

Without looking back to the mirror for fear of losing nerve, he pulled on the vest and then grabbed a thin zip-up hoody in case the sun went in. It was time he started to get out more, and the girls were most definitely going to see to that.

A short ride later and he and Bev were pulling up outside Bedelia's swanky Kensington pad. Adam jumped in the back and Bev playfully honked the horn as Bedelia started towards the car. She quirked a brow at them both before getting into the passenger seat and giving Adam an appreciative smile over her shoulder.

"I like it. And it's good to see you out." There was a slight tone of admonishment there. Although he had seen the girls frequently, he had definitely been avoiding going out socially since getting the surgery. His anxiety had got worse, not better, mainly because he was so caught up in worrying that surgery didn't really fix anything that he couldn't relax about it. Both Bev and Bedders had told him over and over he looked great. He was rarely misgendered now when he *did* go out, his stubble coming in a little more - even if it took weeks on end of no shaving to get there.

Adam knew that the real anxiety lay in his clothing. It always had. His sense of dress hadn't changed much in a long while. He had missed the light vest and delicate cardigans that he saw plenty of queer guys pull off perfectly well and had worn himself until trying to present more masculine. And of course he had been too conscious to wear vests with the binder exposed. Now that he could wear them without that concern he worried they were too effeminate. No matter how many internet memes he read and agreed with about trans guys not having to be the epitome of masculinity, his anxiety told him it didn't apply to him. Having not been "boy" enough for so long, now presenting physically as masculine he was conscious of looking too feminine. Of being misgendered.

He let out a sad sigh at the thought. It often came back to that. He'd had several really shitty experiences with it, especially at work and that one time with that crazy European guy in the bar. It wasn't something that seemed to get easier, he just wanted it to stop happening. Maybe now that he'd had top surgery it would be better. Unfortunately, sometimes it was hard to hope.

Bedelia clearly read his look in the mirror she had pulled down to reapply her lipstick, and interpreted it uncannily, so well did she know him -

"Stop it. You look amazing. You don't look *girly*, you look like you. And you are Adam and Adam is a fucking delight, so don't you dare be down on

11

yourself." She looked at him so sternly that he knew she was completely serious and maybe that was what made him grin so hard in response.

"Thanks Bedders."

Her look turned cold. "Don't fucking call me that." she glared at him before snapping the mirror back up.

Bev snorted a laugh and started the engine.

*

Elias picked at the sandwich and put it back on the buffet table, it did not look appetising in the least. British food could be very strange, and they ate a surprising amount of curry. Fish and chips was usually a fair option but he was put off that his local chip shop also served deep fried chocolate bars. These were a complicated people, culinarily speaking, and Elias wasn't sure he had the time for it. He certainly didn't have time for egg mayonnaise and ham and cheese sandwiches that sat, curling, in the afternoon sun.

He wiped a hand over his brow - starting to sweat a little now. He had opted for his favourite suit - cream linen with a white shirt - but now had sweated so much he couldn't take off his jacket for fear of the state of his shirt underneath. British weather was… ridiculous. How could the sun be so intense when it wasn't even so very warm?

"Having fun Elias?" Jack Crawford slapped a hand on his back that nearly knocked the air out of him.

"E-lee-as." He corrected the pronunciation of his name for what must have been the millionth time since arriving in England.

"Yeah, yeah right." Jack agreed with a nod. Elias narrowed his eyes wondering why his boss had come to talk to him. Wasn't it enough that he had made the effort to come to this rather dull garden party when he could have been enjoying the sun in the park or perhaps having a drink with friends? Yes there were definitely other people in his life he could spend time with that were more than just colleagues. That was very true!

"How have you settled in though, hm? You've been with us a few months now and… I just worry that you're not meshing with the team. You get along with everyone right?" Jack looked a little concerned and Elias's immediate thought was to tell him that he did not *mesh* with the team because they were all idiots.

He shrugged. "I'm sure this party is the perfect opportunity to know them better."

Jack grinned in response and gave another nod. Perhaps he had missed the sarcasm in his tone? Elias was about to correct him and let him know exactly what he thought of the other staff at the small publishers when one of them - Brian - called out-

"Heads up!"

Jack turned as the rugby ball hurtled from the wide expanse of the lawn towards them, standing at the table on the patio. He raised his hand to ward it off, clearly not realising he had a cup grasped in it, until the cup and it's contents went flying at Elias and drenched his face and upper body in sticky rum and coke.

"Shit." Brian cursed as Elias turned his glare on him and his even more annoying boyfriend Jimmy, who he'd had the misfortune of meeting several times before and he got no less annoying for exposure.

Brian turned and ran to the other side of the garden - apparently to hide - Jimmy hesitating before he followed at speed whilst several other party goers around them snickered.

Elias huffed and pulled his hanky from his top pocket to wipe his face, only to find it soaked through with the brownish fluid.

"Shit, I'm sorry, let me just… there's napkins, hang on…" Jack was fussing around the table trying to grab the napkins but Elias didn't wait. He turned and stormed towards the house feeling humiliated.

The backdoor lead into the kitchen where Jack's wife Bella stood with a small gathering of people fixing some drinks.

"Bathroom." Elias demanded indignantly.

"Upstairs…" Bella looked him over and raised a brow, everyone falling silent around her as Elias huffed again and headed out of the kitchen door and found the stairs along the corridor. He stomped up them and was glad to at least see the bathroom was marked with a little sign.

As he tried the door it swung open and he fell into the young man who had apparently been exiting the facilities.

"Shit sorry." and then a concerned. "Are you ok?"

Elias's jaw clenched and he tried to hold back the tears but it was too late. He pushed into the bathroom and dropped onto the lidded toilet, letting his head fall into his hands and unable to stop the little sob.

He waited for the door to close but instead heard a mumbled - "shit… you're not… ugh. Fuck."

And then the door did close but the man had obviously not left because then there was a heavy sigh and Elias felt a hand on his shoulder.

"Are you ok?" The man asked again, this time a tender edge to the tone.

Elias choked out a sob and the tears started to fall.

"I hate it here, everyone is rude and I have done nothing to them, and yet they are mean to me like they are children. I should go back to Denmark. Gabriel was right, it was stupid to move to London. And now I am here and my best suit is ruined by stupid child-men." The words tumbled out, gurgled here and there.

"Shh, shh, you're fine." The hands were on his knees then as the man dropped to his haunches in front of him. "You're gonna be just fine. Honestly, we can sort out this suit. It's too hot for a jacket anyways, you'll be fine without." The hands on his knees gave a comforting rub and then left a cool spot when the man stood again. "Here, shrug out of it."

Hands were on his shoulders and he sniffed as he took his head out of his hands and let the man help him out of the jacket. He looked down at his shirt, which seemed to have escaped the worst of it, as he heard water start pouring. At least the smell of alcohol seemed strong enough to hide any smell of his body odour there might be.

He sniffed again and wiped at his eyes as he studied the slight man's back. He was scrubbing Elias's jacket in the sink, his muscular shoulders surprisingly delicate in the vest he was wearing.

"Thank you." Elias stumbled over the words. He was probably the only nice person Elias had actually met since moving to London. "Londoners are very rude so I'm surprised to have someone be so kind."

The other man chuckled and turned off the faucet before turning to Elias with a grin. "Ever thought they might just be reacting to you being an asshole?"

Elias tried to reply but spluttered an indignant string of vowels in place of the words he couldn't find.

The other man was still smiling at him, a strangely fond look. "Damn. You know, I can't believe I had such anxiety over our last meeting when it turns out you're just a little baby bear."

"I… I'm not a… That is ridiculous. I'm…" he didn't know which to be most insulted by, being called a baby or compared to a large hairy animal.

"Ok, maybe not a bear." The other man chuckled. "Maybe a bull. You're certainly bull-headed, and I wouldn't let you loose in a china shop."

"What are you talking about? You make no sense at all!" Elias stood and snatched back his jacket.

The man seemed unsettled by the action and he wrapped his arms around his chest. "I… I was… I was just trying to…"

Elias cocked his head and studied the man for the first time. The vulnerable look on the strangely beautiful face sparked his memory and he felt his face flush with heat.

*

"You ok?" Bev grabbed Adam's arm as he tried to pass through the kitchen and back out into the fresh air, snatching his hoody from the back of a stool as he went.

"Fine." Adam replied curtly as he brushed her off. "I don't feel great. I'm gonna get a taxi home."

"No… I'll take you." Bev fell into step beside him and they made it out into the sunshine.

Adam stopped and took in a deep breath, trying to calm himself before shrugging the hoody on and zipping it up in one swift motion.

"What happened?" Bev took hold of his hand and he squeezed it.

"I'm just… my anxiety, I… I can't." His chest felt tight, he felt bound and dysphoric and exposed. "I shouldn't have worn this." He pulled his hand away to wrap his arms around himself again, feeling so completely out of place. It was starting to get hard not blaming Jimmy for shitty social situations considering he invited them to this party.

"It's ok." Bev told him, knowing better than to try to convince him he looked fine, instead she somehow made herself huge and enveloped him in a hug, pressing his own arms against him.

"I'm sorry."

"You're fine. Party hugs are my favourite."

Adam's chest was loosened by the chuckle that escaped. He felt himself relax a little into Bev until he heard a voice behind him.

"Did I upset you?"

He stiffened in Bev's arms. *Yes* the asshole had upset him. He had tried to help the man and had instead been scrutinised *again*. Been greeted with a frown and a glance at his chest and a deeper frown. The words echoed in his head and he shuddered - *"Are you really a man?"*

"I didn't mean to upset you. I was surprised because you used to be a woman."

He felt Bev stiffen then and practically heard her teeth grinding. She turned them and let go of Adam so that she had effectively stepped in front of him, hiding him behind her. "Look, asshole, why don't you go and educate yourself on how to behave in polite society and just f-"

"Woah, what's going on here?" Brian's boss, Jack, who was hosting the party had wandered over, drink in hand. Adam felt embarrassed and hated the attention that was being drawn to him and the situation. He wasn't sure if everyone was watching them or if it was just his imagination but he felt humiliated and exposed either way.

"It's… It's ok. I don't feel well, Bev is taking me home." Adam made the effort to stand straighter as he said it and tugged at Bev's hand.

Jack looked like he was about to speak but Bev turned and started towards the gate, hand still in his as she dragged Adam along with her. He pulled his hoodie as tight to him as possible. Wishing he'd brought a scarf too, feeling everything within him falling apart.

Once he was in the passenger seat of the car he put his head in his hands and began to cry.

*

Bev held out a glass of water for him and he took it.

Adam gulped down the cooling liquid, at least going someway to combat the heat of the thick, woollen jumper he now wore over pyjamas. A comfort, and worth the sweating as he curled into his overstuffed sofa. Bev dropped down next to him with a sigh.

"You ok?"

He turned to her and frowned. "I love you, but stop fucking asking me. I'm fine… I'll be fine. I just…" he let out a long sigh. "I'm just exhausted with it all. It wasn't just that guy, it's everything. Getting comfortable with my body when it's constantly changing, having to deal with people on top of that who just have no fucking clue…" he trailed off and shook his head, exasperated. "It doesn't matter. It's just… I thought, urgh. I felt bad that he was upset, and I was just trying to be nice. He couldn't help but be a dick and I'm fed up of that shit. Aren't I dealing with enough without having to put up with rude, ignorant shits?"

"I know sweetie." Bev rubbed his arm and then gave it a squeeze. "Do you want me to hang out for a bit?"

Adam shook his head. He already felt like an ass for dragging her away from the party, besides he found it easier to be alone sometimes and this was definitely one of those times. He didn't want the fuss, as much as he equally didn't want to get too lost in his own thoughts.

Despite how much more comfortable he felt since having top surgery, it wasn't exactly an easy and straightforward adjustment to make after spending years trying, and halfway succeeding in trying to love and accept your body to then change it. Some days it fucked with his mind almost as much as his lessening dysphoria did. With his panic over outfits, this had already started to be one of those days before he'd run into that loon again.

Bev stood and leaned in to kiss his forehead before she said her goodbyes and headed out the door.

Adam clenched his jaw. No it wasn't just that guy, but it didn't help that the man tore him down each time they had met, even if it was unintentional. And... he wasn't going to stand for it again. Next time he was going to steel his nerve and give as good as he got. Channel some of that forthright asshole he had been before the anxiety and dysphoria had got so bad. That was the goal wasn't it? Get back to the old Adam, the Adam he had been before he *was* Adam. Over-sexed, over-sassed and ready to take on the damn world. The Adam he had been before everything had fallen apart and he had remade himself to become whole, finally.

Yes, if he ever ran into that idiot again, things would go very fucking differently!

*

Elias threw the slightly less stained jacket onto the bed as soon as he walked into the bedsit. He was angry and upset and confused and that seemed to happen every time he ran into the confusing man who... confused him.

This time it had been more difficult to associate him with the woman he had met those several months ago, but in some ways that confused Elias even more.

He shouldn't dwell on it of course, they may never meet again and that would be for the best - she...*he*... was certainly very rude and a tad violent. Elias would never dream of acting how this person did. Best that he steer well clear of the unstable stranger.

That resolved, he had a shower, came twice, and then called Gabriel and asked - "If I met a woman and now she is a man, should I call her *he?*"

Gabriel, as was his way, had of course talked to him like he was a child. And then given him several long words to google.

3

Soho Square was getting cold as the clouds started to blot the afternoon sun. The bench beneath him almost damp from it, but Adam savoured the fresh air whilst he still could. He knew it was going to be a while before he was able to get out and about again. With top surgery he had healed up fine and felt pretty healthy after a couple of weeks, but mentally it had been hard to get back into things. He had never been happier to go freelance from work, at least working from home had been no problem. This time around he wasn't sure what the mental impact would be - maybe more considering the surgery, maybe less as it wasn't something that he had the same sort of dysphoria and discomfort as he had his chest.

He took in a deep breath and released it slowly. Tomorrow, more surgery, another step on this journey. Another step towards fulfilling the potential of *being* Adam.

Adam centred himself and stood. He had plans. Groceries had been delivered, he was all set to hole up and recover in his flat - all he needed were some DVD boxsets to keep him company. So, grab a coffee and then make his way to the shops. Plan. A good way to stay focused and keep his mind off the morning.

He took a step and was immediately hit by a wall of force out of nowhere. He toppled back, about to fall, when large strong hands grasped him and pulled him upright. They held him close for a moment whilst he took a breath, and then he looked up as they allowed him to move back.

"Sorry, I…" the man stopped short and Adam was sure his moustache twitched slightly just before a blush rose on his cheeks.

"You…" Adam had no words. It had been well over a year since the garden party where he had run into this guy. *Elias*, Bedelia had informed him, a Dane working at Crawford's publishers, translating tourism guides. She had got the information from Brian and Jimmy who had declared him *a total weirdo*.

Strangely that had struck Adam. How many people had described him as such when he was growing up? When he was finding himself? Even now, maybe more so now? Or at least his paranoia told him such. He had developed a sort of sympathy and wondered how he might react if they met again. What was it that made this man a weirdo? And who was anyone to judge it?

But they hadn't ever met again. It wasn't like they usually ran in the same circles, each meeting had been pretty much a fluke. And after a while Adam had put the whole thing out of his mind.

Until today.

As the man tried to stammer something, still holding his arms, Adam allowed a smile.

"It's ok. You're in a hurry? Sorry I just stood up from the bench without looking, I-"

"No, no, it's my fault. I'm sorry. I should have been more vigilant." Elias blushed and then seemed to realise his hands were still grasping Adam's arms. His eyes widened and he let go. "I'm sorry, sorry." He held up his hands in placation and looked for a moment like he was about to bolt. And maybe that would be for the best given their last encounters, but…

Adam wasn't one for hard luck cases. He wasn't cold, but he wasn't exactly the cuddly type. He was strong and hard and standoffish because he'd had to be. And yet, hearing this man called a weirdo jarred something within him. Weren't they all weirdos in their own way?

"It's Elias isn't it? You work with Brian?" Adam said quickly before he had chance to run, and it worked, the man's shoulders eased back and his face formed a sort of scowl. Adam laughed. "I'll take that as a yes… he's a bit of an acquired taste."

"He… yes, he is." Elias looked for all the world like he had plenty to say on the subject of Brian Zeller but seemed polite enough not to. More than Brian and Jimmy had been. But then they were such gossips. And Brian was a bit of an asshole even if he was a nice guy underneath it all – perhaps he might have that in common with Elias.

"I was just going to get a coffee. Did you want to… oh, were you going somewhere? You were in a hurry… on a late lunch?"

"I like to walk briskly." Elias answered, still looking a little flustered but the blush was fading. "I have finished work for the day and I have already had coffee."

"Tea then? I just meant… If you wanted to sit down and drink? Together?" Adam winced on the inside. Making friends was even harder than picking someone up, and he'd been adept at that at one time.

"Together?" Elias seemed taken aback.

"Just to, um, be friendly? I know we keep getting off on the wrong foot and if I'm going to run into you every now and then I'd like it if we were at least friendly?"

Elias gave a curt nod and Adam pointed across the square.

"I was going to the coffee shop over there. That ok?"

Another nod and Elias fell into step at his side. He seemed like he wanted to say something but was unable to find the words. Either way, something felt heavy between them, like dark clouds about to release the drought-quenching rain.

*

Elias was startled by the burst of laughter from his companion, tears in the man's eyes as he laughed at something amusing Elias had said. Or at least, Elias had hoped it was amusing, not everyone understood his humour. The laughter echoed around the tiny coffee shop and seemed to cause the waiter at the counter and one other patron in a window seat, to smile at its infectiousness.

"Oh yeah, that sounds exactly like something Brian would do!" Adam, as he turned out to be called, wiped tears from his eyes as he tried to quell his laughter.

Elias smiled, almost a little unnerved that his joking about his colleague had gone down so well. A silly concern of course because he was very humorous and should expect at least some people of good taste to appreciate that as Adam clearly did. Adam was obviously more appreciative of good humour than most Londoners he had encountered.

It was so strange sitting with this man and talking so nicely. Elias didn't make friends easily, mostly because other people were often not very bright or witty and many more not worth his time. But Adam was... nice.

"I like that you have that cruel edge to your humour." Adam grinned. "Not enough people can be funny and harsh like that without actually being a complete asshole."

Elias blinked. "I am not cruel. I'm just honest."

Adam snickered and sipped at his coffee. It was his second refill and Elias was on his third iced tea, not that it was very nice in this cafe - he would have to insist they go somewhere better next time. It occurred to him that he would like there to be a next time with his new friend and so he knew there was something he had to broach first.

"Adam, my brother told me I was rude and I should say sorry. Not that I believe I did anything wrong, I think I acted as anyone would when you were being so confusing. But... I've read lots of things on the internet..." his words trailed off a little, caught under a blue gaze as open as the ocean.

"Ok..." Adam seemed to be waiting for something.

"You accept my apology. Good." Elias was pleased. He was clearly right that this had been the best thing to do.

Adam chuckled again. "You... you actually didn't apologise Elias."

"I certainly did." Elias blustered at both the words and then amused look of his new friend. "And it wasn't my fault you were so confusing to me. I am sure I am not the only person you confused."

Adam's smile tweaked a little and he took in a deep breath and released it slowly. "Elias, I like you, but I stand by what I said about you being bull-headed. And yes, I remember that's what I said to you, because yes every encounter I've had with you is etched in my brain for all the wrong reasons." He stopped and sipped his coffee, eyes burning into Elias over the rim of the cup. "Until now." He muttered and looked at his mug as he set it back down.

"I see... well, as you accepted my apology perhaps we can start over." Elias said firmly and was rewarded with a lopsided smirk.

"Ok, here's the deal. I accept your apology if you can promise me you really understand what upset me and-"

"You were upset because I said you were a woman." Elias finished with certainty.

The smile was gone then and Adam was clearly clenching his jaw. His words were tight when he replied - "Not quite. Do you understand what transgender is?"

"Of course, I'm not an idiot. I can read the internet. I understand you used to be female and then you... transferred."
"Transitioned."

"Yes, as I said." Elias huffed. "It is no wonder it confuses people, but I'm not confused anymore."

"You're not?" There was a slight grin again and Elias felt strangely rewarded by it.

"No." He shrugged. "You were female, and now you are male, and you are Adam. Only an idiot wouldn't understand that and as I said I'm not an idiot."

Adam's lips did twitch into a grin then and his eyes widened a little. Perhaps he was amused though Elias was sure that wasn't funny at all. He really wasn't an idiot.

"Of course, it was probably more confusing because you are very beautiful." Elias tried to keep the reprimand out of his tone.

"You think I'm beautiful?" Adam grinned and gave a salacious wink.

Elias blustered and felt his face heat as he was caught off guard by the flirtation. "In the way a man can be beautiful I suppose. It's not like you are the only beautiful man. I myself am often complimented on how handsome I am!"

"Oh yes, very…" Adam winked again and Elias opened and closed his mouth a few times but nothing came out. Adam broke into laughter then. "I'm just teasing you Elias. You're not my type. I just wanted to watch you squirm."

Elias huffed to show his lack of amusement. Of course he wasn't Adam's type - Adam was a man and Elias wasn't a woman, so why would that even be in question? Elias shook it off, resigning himself to the fact that Adam may continue to be somewhat confusing but it was worth putting up with for another iced tea sometime. Speaking of which, he lifted his glass again and swallowed the last of the bitter tea.

"This tea really isn't very nice. I think tomorrow I should take you to Nadine's - the cafe across the street from Crawford's. I finish at 3pm then also."

Adam raised his eyebrows so high they almost disappeared into his hair. "You want to do this again then? Friendly drinks?"

"I suppose so, if I have nothing better to do. As I said, I am free tomorrow afternoon around the same time." Elias gave a dismissive wave of his hand. He could fit Adam in tomorrow, and it might be nice to see him again so soon, but he wasn't going to go to trouble over it of course.

"Tomorrow, ah… I can't." Adam's brows fell into a frown.

Elias clenched his jaw at the rejection and shrugged. "Well, that's just fine. I'm not sure you would like Nadine's anyway."

"But, maybe another time?" Adam offered and Elias screwed his face up at the thought of the offer coming from a place of pity.

"I don't need fair weather friends-"

"Elias, I can't tomorrow, I'm checking in for surgery." Adam rudely interrupted him.

"Surgery? Are you sick?" Elias narrowed his eyes, he didn't look sick.

Adam glared at him. "No... I'm not sick."

"Then why do you need surgery?" Elias was utterly bamboozled by the obvious excuse to avoid seeing him.

Adam's gaze continued to be hard and a little disbelieving. "Look it's personal, not everyone wants to discuss what surgery they are undertaking."

"What surgery are you *undertaking?*" Elias eyed him suspiciously.

Adam threw up his hands, startling Elias a little. "Do you want to look at my fucking medical charts? What is wrong with you? Can't you see this is making me uncomfortable and I don't want to discuss my fucking lower surgery with you?!"

Elias frowned, his eyes narrowing. "I take it back. You are very rude, I don't think I want to have tea with you tomorrow, or ever."

"Well... fine!" Adam was on his feet then and grabbing his jacket before Elias could say anything more. "I'm not going to have time to get any boxsets now and it's going to be boring as fucking hell and I blame you." Adam stabbed a finger at him, just short of his nose, and then turned and walked out - leaving the cafe door swinging behind him.

The waiter looked over from the counter and winced. "Oh buddy, you really fucked up."

*

Adam cursed when his doorbell buzzed. He really should give Bev a key, for the time being at least. She was popping in most nights after work to see if he needed anything. He'd been out of hospital two weeks and was still on doctor's orders to take things easy. He practically lived on his sofa and was working his way through the boxsets that Bev had dropped by. He'd watched so much Mad Men that he wasn't sure where one season ended and the other began at this point.

He shuffled from the sofa and made his way to the door, trying to school the scowl that Bev didn't deserve. It easily morphed into a confused frown when he opened the door.

"Don't blame me." Bev protested, hands up in defence, "he insisted."

"How…" Adam started but couldn't find the words as Bev moved passed him into the flat, leaving Elias standing on the door step and looking at him uncomfortably.

"I sent you flowers." Elias told him before looking down at his feet. "To say sorry and I hoped you were well, after… um."

Adam turned and looked at Bev. "What is he doing here?"

Bev was picking at a bunch of grapes she appeared to have brought with her. She shrugged before finally swallowing a mouthful and replying - "Brian gave him my number and he called me."

Adam scrubbed a hand over his face. He really didn't need this, he was exhausted and felt like shit physically and mentally. He wanted to close the door in the man's face but was too polite for that.

"So you brought him here?" Adam's emotions reeled between flustered and pissed. He really didn't want to be around anyone right now, didn't want to be seen until he was ready to be. He couldn't believe Bev wouldn't have realised that.

Bev's face dropped as she realised she had made a mistake, and Elias interjected - "I asked her. I wanted to… I sent you flowers."

"I didn't get any fucking flowers." Adam near shouted and then walked off at a pace a little more painful than he'd have liked, leaving the door open. Adam scooted along the corridor and shut himself in the bathroom. He took a breath, leaning against the counter and looking down into the sink. He wasn't sure how long he'd been in there, at least a few minutes when Bev knocked on the door and spoke through the hollow panels –

"Adam baby, I'm sorry. I didn't think. Look, he means well. He asked Brian for my number so he could talk to you, but I didn't want to give him your details so I told him you were in hospital. He said he knew… and I don't know maybe I misread everything? I let him know which ward and he says he sent flowers but didn't hear from you so he was worried. He kept calling and I… I just felt bad for the guy. I'm sorry. I can ask him to leave? I can leave too?"

"I didn't get any flowers." Adam muttered just loud enough to be heard. He wasn't sure why the very thought of that irked him other than to give him something to fixate on in this ridiculous situation. Why wouldn't this guy just leave him be?

"Ok... I don't know what happened with the flowers. Do you want me to-" Adam moved as she talked and opened the door, cutting her off. "It doesn't matter. I hate cut flowers, I'd have preferred chocolates." He knew he sounded petulant but Bev smiled and took hold of his hands.

"I can ask him to go? He's just sat on the sofa."

"It's fine." Adam sighed and headed back to the small living room.

Elias stood when they came back in, fidgeting before holding out a box of chocolates.

"If you didn't like the flowers perhaps you might like these? Even so, it would have been polite to thank me for the flowers even if you hated them."

Adam rolled his eyes but couldn't find it in himself to be mad or frustrated with the man, it seemed such a waste of energy. "I didn't get them." Adam repeated again as he took the chocolates, a small smile tweaking his lips at the thought Elias might as well have read his mind. "Thanks for these... and the flowers."

Elias gave a nod of acknowledgement and then sat back down.

"Ok, well. I'm going to head over to the chip shop and grab some food for us. Fish and chips for three?" She shot Adam a questioning glance and he shrugged then nodded. She returned the nod and then turned to Elias. "Just... don't go upsetting him or I will be having words with you when I get back."

Elias looked taken aback and practically scowled after Bev which tweaked a smile at Adam's lips. This guy really was just on his own planet and yet... he had tried to apologise in his own way, he had realised he had upset Adam with his words and actions and had tried to correct his ignorance. He really had made an effort, and the truth was not everyone in Adam's life had. Elias was as confusing to him as he was to Elias and there was something endearing and vastly entertaining about that.

When the door clicked shut Adam moved to the sofa and gingerly lowered himself back down into his nest of cushions, the opposite end to Elias.

"You're hard work Elias, but I guess you're alright."

Elias looked up and gave him a broad smile that lit his entire face.

4

"You changed your clothes again." Elias's eyes followed him into the room as he moved to stand next to where Elias sat on the sofa. "I thought you were just taking a long time in the bathroom."

Adam knew Elias well enough now to ignore the slight tinge of annoyance in his tone. The man seemed indignant about something at any given time, it was nothing personal he knew. If anything it had become annoyingly endearing to him.

"I... I didn't like it." Adam said and Elias gave a nod of understanding. In the months since they had become friends they had both gotten used to each other's little quirks. Elias's inappropriate comments and Adam's occasional dysphoria, amongst the many *many* other things between them that made up who they were.

"Well. You look very nice." Elias commented, looking away and acting as though he hadn't just given Adam a compliment. Adam grinned at Elias's comment that he would swear wasn't just an attempt to be supportive, but Adam knew different.

Adam looked down. The t-shirt was baggy but the skinny jeans tight, ending in clumpy boots. He paired it with a light scarf and grabbed his jacket, yeah, this was better than what he had on before. This was *Adam*. "You ready?"

Elias nodded and moved from the sofa and grabbed his own jacket.

"You look nice too Elias." Adam smiled and enjoyed the reddening of the man's cheeks.

It was Thursday late afternoon so they ended up at Nadine's as usual - the nice little cafe that Elias liked. They sat reading and sipping their drinks in the comfortable and companionable silence they enjoyed around each other. Elias was the most sedate of his friends really. He loved them all, but the peace of the man's company was always welcome, he felt calmed and comforted by it. Elias felt solid and reliable in a different way than his other friends. Sometimes it felt like he had known him so long that it was strange to think Elias never knew him before the transition. He was glad of it, it made him feel more whole. Elias had only ever been *Adam's* friend.

Adam to Elias on the other hand… Adam was pretty sure he was Elias's only friend in London. Something he was trying to remedy by including Elias with his friends. He was an acquired taste, but not unlikeable. Even Bedelia seemed to manage to get past the surface and enjoy that Elias knew at least as many languages as she did.

"Are you still up for tomorrow night?" Adam asked.

That roused Elias from the book he was reading. "Hmm?"

"Tomorrow, the pub with Bev and Bedelia. Don't worry, Zeller and Jimmy can't make it." Adam grinned.

"Yes. Okay." Elias replied gruffly.

Adam frowned. "You don't have to if you don't want?"

"No I…" Elias huffed. "I like spending time with you. Your friends are hard work."

Adam laughed at that - as he had when Bev and Bedelia had said the same of Elias.

"Bedelia is interesting, but a snob. Bev is… very forthright. I'm not sure it suits her." Elias grumbled before looking back down at his book.

Adam laughed. "You'd deserve for me to tell Bev that you said that. You truly have no filter. Sometimes I don't know whether to find you amusing or offensive." Elias's features flipped to a well-worn indignation and Adam laughed again. "I just want you to enjoy yourself, you seem so lost in London."

Elias's eyes narrowed. "I'm fine." Elias bristled with his usual defensiveness.

"I didn't mean… just that. Well, have you thought about dating? I'm sure Bev would drag you along to one of those speed dating things she often attends." Adam smiled as sweetly as he could in order to curb any overreaction from Elias. It worked as the man's face went from near bluster back down to indignation.

"I can get my own dates. I'm not like you, having dates every week with different people. Which isn't healthy you know? I hope you are careful" He paused thoughtfully and then added. "But I suppose I can understand, now you are Adam you can date in a way you couldn't before." He nodded. "But that's you. I want to find something meaningful or nothing at all."

Adam was sort of touched by his words. And it was true, he'd seen several different guys but it never really went anywhere. He'd had a date a couple of weeks ago that went really well and they might go out again, but he was cautious. The few on *Grindr* that had swiped right when they saw he was trans weren't always prepared for the reality. Most dates started with questions about his genitalia, and well, that was just fucking weird and rude. What was everyone's obsession with transgender body parts? His stock reply was - *Unless you're planning on fucking me, it's none of your damn business!*

That had ended a few dates. The ones that had gone further and even resulted in sex, just seemed to… fizzle. There was a lot of baggage - real or imagined - that these fellas seemed to feel came with dating a trans guy. And quite frankly if they didn't think Adam was worth it, *they* for sure as shit weren't. His confidence was growing, he was comfortable with who he was and how he presented himself to the world. He wasn't going to take on anyone that thought differently to that.

"But you have to put yourself out there, how will you find something meaningful if you don't? When was your last date?" Adam asked gently, really just wanting Elias to have someone other than just him, as close as they had become.

Elias let out a sigh as though he had given up trying to not have this conversation. Adam managed to hide a smile at that, Elias certainly knew how tenacious Adam could be.

"Adam… there's…" Elias went red faced as he trailed off.

"What?" Adam sat forward, concerned at the flurry of emotion across Elias's face. "Are you okay?"

"Yes. I just… I have a condition. It makes it hard to date. Women don't like it. It's difficult to discuss." Elias's tone was quiet but accusatory - falling back onto his offensive defense.

"Okay… well, what is it? Can I help? Have you seen a doctor?" Adam reached across the table and put his hand on Elias's arm to comfort the man who now looked on the verge of tears.

With that touch Elias jumped up and ran to the bathroom, clearly sobbing.

"Shit." Adam muttered in his wake.

He gave Elias a few minutes before following him in and finding him in one of the two stalls. His low and pitiful sobs clear.

"We have to stop meeting in bathrooms." Adam joked of their earlier encounters, but that didn't seem to stop or even lessen Elias's sobs. "Please Elias. I'm your friend, talk to me. It's not like you don't know plenty of personal shit about me? I want to help."

Adam let out a sigh and leaned back against the sink a moment before the door swung open revealing a flustered and red-faced Elias. His belt and trousers were undone but he, thankfully, wasn't exposing himself. Adam didn't even know what the hell to think or where to look as Elias grabbed his hard - and apparently sizeable - dick through the material.

"This is the problem." He sobbed.

"Oh… Elias…" Adam felt desperately sad for the distress his friend seemed to be in. He wanted to reach out and comfort the man but was aware this might not be wholly appropriate.

"It's a form of Priapism, it is hereditary. It could be worse." Elias sobbed as he wiped his tears on his sleeve. "At least it goes when I relieve myself. At least for a while. But… it is worse when things arouse me. And I have no control over what arouses me. *You've* even aroused me… before."

Adam felt a cold stab go through him at those words. *Before.* Before what? Before they were friends? Before he realised Adam was a man? The idea of Elias being aroused by him as a woman made something within him hurt. Something he had to put aside and maybe think on later, right now his friend needed him.

"Okay, well what can I do? Should we get you home? Should I... uh, leave you to it in here? Don't worry about dating, there's no pressure. Let's deal with one thing at a time."

Elias nodded solemnly. "I need to... could you wait at the table? So I can..." he was reddening by the minute, unable to meet Adam's gaze as his cock leaked precum through the material of his trousers.

"Oh! Sure, yeah. I'll, I'll just..." Adam didn't finish, returning to the table instead. He tried to ignore his own slight hardness and dismiss it as just the idea of such a big cock. Maybe even jealousy perhaps? It wasn't like he was into Elias like *that.*

*

"Are you sure he's coming?" Bev said as they ordered four drinks for the three of them.

"Yeah, he said he would." Adam didn't sound convinced even to his own ears. He bought Elias's pint anyway.

The events of the previous day had been awkward. After Elias had returned from the bathroom they had gone back to his place and he had been clearly uncomfortable at Adam being there, so Adam had left. They hadn't talked since but Elias hadn't text to cancel or anything.

"Everything okay with you guys?" Bev asked as she carried her own pint and Bedelia's wine over to their booth.

"Yeah. He just... he has health issues he's a bit self-conscious about." Adam said, then huffed with some amusement. "Which I can empathise with, right? I mean, it's not the same, obviously. But I guess... there are times he doesn't quite feel comfortable in his body either."

"Okay." Bev gave a comforting smile. "I was worried."

"Why were you worried? You don't even like the guy that much." Adam smiled.

"No, but you do. I don't want… I don't know. I want it to work out for the best, whatever that is." She downed half her pint.

"What does that mean? What are you talking about?" Adam felt like he was really missing something. He looked to Bedelia who clearly knew what Bev was getting at but shrugged, in her *I'm not getting involved* way.

"You know… you *like* him. I don't know if he's gay or what? Or whether it's-"

"Woah, Bev, what the fuck are you talking about?" Adam felt a chill sweat rising all over his skin.

"Just… I don't want you to get hurt if it doesn't work out."

Adam's jaw dropped. "Bev, we're not together. He's just my friend. I mean… you know I've been dating. You know I've been seeing people? What-"

"I… I just thought you were saying that because you didn't want us to know?" Bev looked nervously at Adam and then to Bedelia.

Bedelia shrugged and raised an eyebrow at Bev "Don't look at me, I told you they weren't together."

"Who is together?"

The sound of Elias's voice behind him set Adam on edge. He didn't like Elias like *that*! And Elias wasn't gay. Where the fuck was Bev even getting all this from? Probably some shit Zeller was spouting. If that turned out to be the case he would smack him upside the head. Gossipy bitch!

"No one." Adam turned and smiled, before sliding across the booth so Elias could sit. "Bev just gossiping as per usual."

Elias frowned. "You shouldn't do that you know. Gossiping is very rude." He admonished and Bedelia let out a chuckle at Bev's red face.

Bev downed the rest of her drink and got up, heading back towards the bar. Both Adam and Bedelia chuckled before Bedelia swigged back the last of her glass and followed Bev.

Elias frowned. "Those women drink a lot. It's not very ladyli- oh, I mean…" Elias started to fluster and Adam smiled.

"It's ok Elias. Please don't tread on eggshells around me. My gender has nothing to do with how much I do or don't drink. It's about how I feel." Adam spoke softly, not the first time he'd had to reassure his new friend in this way. And the fact was, he didn't even mind. It wasn't like some of the assholes at work who still dead-named him, purposely it often seemed. Elias was trying and Adam was always going to appreciate that.

"Yes." Elias nodded. "I know." He looked contrite even if he didn't voice it.

Adam shook his head. "It's fine, honestly." He put a hand on Elias's forearm and felt the strong muscles beneath.

Badminton

He had joined a club locally, it was something he'd enjoyed back home. Maybe Adam should join too. He hadn't played any sports in years. Too many bad high school memories, too conscious of the clothing. Too hard to deal with the dysphoria of bouncing breasts that apparently no sports bra could compensate for. Maybe now he would feel different, especially with Elias there-

"Hey, Adam! How are you?"

Adam had been lost in thought as Elias had quietly sipped at his beer, apparently unphased by Adam's hand on his arm until the man - Josh - interrupted and Elias shifted his arm at the same time Adam withdrew his hand.

"Oh, Josh. Hey. Um, yeah I'm good." Adam could feel heat rising in his cheeks and the familiar stirrings of the first panic attack in a long while.

"You never called-" Josh was all smiles and the tone was pleasant if slightly accusatory.

"No, shit. I guess I didn't. Sorry, I... I didn't mean to lead you on." Adam was growing more tense by the moment, more so when Elias turned to look at him, clearly confused by the interaction.

"What's happening? Are you okay?" Elias asked, concerned.

Adam nodded and gave a weak smile.

"Oh... oh, sorry. Fuck. My bad, I didn't realise you were with someone... shit. Well, it was good to see you." Josh spoke hurriedly, eyeing up Elias, and then turned and walked off.

Adam let out a deep breath and shuddered, his anxiety spiking. He wanted to curl into a ball and cry.

"Of course you can see me, you aren't blind. What was he talking about? Some people are so strange." Elias's reliable indignation drew a smile from Adam, even calmed him a little. Reliable and dependable friend.

"He meant... He thought I am seeing someone new and that's why I wasn't interested." Adam explained, feeling the better for it, pushing the emotions out rather than holding them in.

"Interested in what? Is this a lost in translation thing?" Elias asked, using a phrase Adam had used with him several times over the months.

Adam laughed, feeling the tightness ease. "No, I... I went on a couple of dates with him. But it was before lower surgery and... I saw a few guys back then and didn't tell them I was trans. Josh was nice, it might have even gone somewhere but I was too scared. I couldn't tell him... I didn't want to be rejected. And I felt weird, like I was misleading people, or lying. Because as much as people want to say that it shouldn't make a difference. It does." Adam sighed, feeling it all pour out of him. He'd never even really told the girls all of this. "Fact is, no matter how *enlightened* a guy might be, when he takes home another guy, he's expecting that guy to have a dick."

Elias looked slightly stunned and Adam was suddenly aware he may have overshared and made him uncomfortable.

"Adam..." Elias frowned and looked confused. "Are you-"

Bev and Bedelia dropped back into the booth before he could finish the question and Adam wasn't sure whether to be relieved or not about that.

*

Elias fidgeted.

Was Adam gay?

He wasn't sure how to feel about that. After all the day before Adam had... he told Adam about his condition and then he had seen him in the bathroom. Elias swallowed hard.

He wasn't paying attention to the conversation, the three of them laughing about some joke or other. Some silly thing Bev did in her lab, which Elias was sure was not funny at all, because working in a laboratory was a serious matter and she should take it as such. It was only when Adam placed a hand on his that he was pulled out of his reverie with a start.

"Sorry, I... I just need the bathroom." Adam smiled.

Elias nodded and slid out of the booth to let Adam out, before sliding back in again. He watched Adam walk into the crowd, his mind still trying to process this new information about his confusing friend.

"Are you alright Elias?" Bedelia asked.

He looked back at the two women and nodded. "Yes. I'm just... I'm a little confused. About Adam."

Both women frowned then and he could sense there was a feeling of defensiveness in the air. They were clearly worried he would disparage their friend. Which was truly shocking because Adam was his friend too and he was sure he was just as protective as either of them.

"How so?" Bedelia's tone was cool.

"I thought... well, Adam is a man so I thought... that he dated women." Elias's own frown deepened as he voiced his confusion aloud.

"Adam's gay." Bev replied, now wearing a deep frown herself. "How... how did you not know that Adam is gay?"

"Gay for men?" Elias tried to clarify. He thought he had figured Adam out but now it was all jumbled in his head again. "Because… I mean, not gay for women."

Bev groaned and buried her head in her hands whilst Bedelia shook her head with a frown he had seen on his teacher's in school.

"No Elias. Adam is gay for men. Adam is a man, who is gay for other men." Bedelia said firmly, with a cold look.

"I… yes, I know. I'm not an idiot." Elias stated just as firmly. "There's no need to be rude about it." He felt his face reddening.

"What's going on?" Adam was back at the booth and looking between the three of them, worried and confused.

"I… don't like rude people." Elias blurted. He didn't, he couldn't abide them. No.

And yet… he knew that his blustering was something else. He felt bad. He felt terrible that he hadn't understood and that they might tell Adam and he might get upset. He wanted to say something else, but a sob choked out instead.

Elias got to his feet. "I think I will go home. It's late."

"Elias, wait!" Adam called out, but he was already walking. Hurrying as fast as he could through the crowd.

He was out the door and down the street before he let himself cry. He marched home, tears blurring his way, hoping that Adam didn't hate him when the ladies told him what he'd said.

5

"Elias, are you okay? I'm worried. Call me."

*

"Ok, Elias, I thought you might need time to chill? But it's been a week! I don't know what upset you. Please let me help."

*

"Elias, this isn't okay. I gave you a few days to call back and still nothing?! You need to call me back! I'm really worried. I'm going to come over."

*

"Elias so fucking help me if you don't answer this door I will kick it in and you will never get the deposit back on this shithole!"

The door swung open revealing a sheepish looking Elias and Adam's heart swelled and sunk at the same time.

"I was fucking worried about you!" He shouted before he even realised it. "What happened?" He asked, lowering his voice.

Elias stepped aside and let Adam into the bedsit.

"I'm sorry." Elias muttered, his back to Adam.

Adam stopped. He had never heard Elias apologies. He'd heard him talk around apologies in the most amazingly skilful way, but never apologise.

"It's ok. I was just worried. You should have called me back." Adam spoke gently.

"No, I mean-" Elias turned and looked at him, his eyes red and threatening tears. "-for ruining our friendship. I didn't mean to."

"Elias, you... you haven't ruined our friendship. Just talk to me, don't shut me out. What happened? I want to help." Adam wanted to reach for Elias but held back.

"Bev told you, and now you hate me." Elias choked back a sob.

"What are you talking about? What did Bev tell me?" Adam was confused and hurting

"I said something bad about you." Elias near whispered.

Adam's blood ran cold at the thought of Elias doing such a thing, but equally at potentially losing this blossoming friendship.

"What? Bev didn't say anything. They just... Bev and Bedelia said they weren't sure why you were upset." Now that he thought about it there had been something slightly off with them when he got back from the loo, but he'd assumed it was because of the way Elias had left abruptly. "What did you say?" Adam asked quietly.

"I... I was confused. I mean, I understand, but... I wasn't sure I..."

"What did you say Elias?" Adam couldn't keep the tremor of concern from his voice.

"I didn't know you were gay. And I wanted to clarify and I think it sounded wrong. I just wanted to understand if you were gay for men or women."

Adam frowned, a little confused. And then the realisation hit him. "You mean, you weren't sure when they said gay, whether I was a gay man or gay woman?" Something fizzed within Adam - anger, frustration. And then the previous apology slotted in. Adam couldn't just give up on Elias when he was clearly still trying. He'd given many people a lot more chances than he'd had to give Elias and they had barely tried. "Elias, you do understand that I'm a man?"

He held his breath waiting for the answer to a question he already thought he didn't need to ask.

"Yes of course." Elias sobbed, shaking as tears ran down his cheeks. "I'm so sorry. I only see you as Adam, I… I don't even remember why I found you feminine the first time we met. But sometimes… it's not a concept I have been familiar with before. It is odd for me thinking you used to be a woman before. I get confused."

Adam's heart ached and the second apology certainly wasn't lost on him, but also the gushed words. That what confused Elias was not accepting him as a man, but trying to reconcile that he had once been a woman.

"I was surprised. I didn't know you were gay and I wanted to understand. Because you are a man and so I thought you liked women." Elias was crying and it broke Adam's heart but he was still not completely sure of the situation, and he needed to be.

"Do you have a problem with me being gay?" Adam asked coolly. He couldn't could he? He couldn't be ok with Adam being trans but not with him being gay?

"No, no. It's fine… I mean, it's none of my business, I was just surprised. You date so much… I didn't understand that you were dating men and it changes things."

"How?" Adam asked gruffly.

"Well… I have been telling you so often when we sit in the cafe, pointing out the attractive ladies passing by, thinking you were also finding them attractive. Do… Should I point out men as well now?" Elias gave a questioning look through teary eyes. "Or stop altogether? I'm very confused. I've never had a gay friend."

"Oh Elias." Adam's heart swelled as the understanding dawned. "So… you were unsure and felt bad because you thought you might have been making me uncomfortable talking about women?"

"I wanted to make sure, and now I feel even more terrible because I have upset you and made you think I don't understand you are a man, *and* all this time I have been talking about women. And you're such a good friend I didn't-"

Adam interrupted the run on words that were starting to become indiscernible. "Elias, Elias, it's fine." And then he let the light laugh escape that had been swelling within him. It was the first time he had ever heard Elias admit to really feeling bad about something he had said or done - at least without then turning it around into how, in fact, it was someone else's fault altogether.

Elias let out another sob, though it seemed tinged with relief.

"Oh you bloody idiot, come here." Adam smiled and stepped the distance between them and hugged Elias to him.

Elias shook for a moment, more tears, and then let out a sigh. He pulled his arms up around Adam and held him close as they breathed together, both overwhelmed with the sense of relief and recovery. Another chuckle escaped Adam at that relief.

They stood this way for a few minutes. Comfortable and supportive of each other. It felt nice. It was only interrupted when Elias took in a deep, calming breath and then muttered -

"You smell nice."

"Thanks." Adam smiled against Elias's shoulder. "I have a date later."

He wasn't sure which of them froze first, or which one of them pulled away, but he knew they both felt equally awkward and conversation was hard to come by until Adam excused himself so as not to be late for dinner.

*

Adam did smell nice. Elias had thought so on several occasions but he had never been close enough before to really appreciate it fully. Very musky and male, slightly sweaty - which he had pointed out to Adam once before and Adam had explained he often sweated more because of the testosterone. But it wasn't an unpleasant smell. Combined with the always lovely and complementary scents Adam wore, he always smelt very wonderful. At least to Elias, who would admit he was not *au fait* in the judgement of how other men smelled.

Perhaps Adam would be a better judge as he dated men.

The thought struck something within him that he found difficult to find the root of. He would have called it jealousy - after all, he appeared to be Adam's only close male friend and what if a boyfriend would steal that away? But it was absurd to be jealous, after all Elias was a wonderful friend, even if they had had their ups and downs. No boyfriend could replace Elias as Adam's good male friend.

That would be preposterous, he reminded himself as he grabbed his jacket and left the bedsit in search of a hard drink.

It was the bar that he and Adam went to the most, and where he knew Adam often went with Bev and Bedelia, but that wasn't the reason Elias went, of course.

It was true that perhaps Adam might take his date there and Elias, if there were really any competition, could assess the likelihood of being replaced by a love interest... but that wasn't why he was there. No, they had very good beer. He was surely unlikely to find that beer in any of the other local bars.

"Elias!" He recognised Bev's voice and turned to see her sitting with Jimmy Price and Brian Zeller. The thought of joining them was not appealing, but at least he would look less like he was spying on Adam should he appear. And of course, he wasn't spying at all.

Elias nodded in recognition and collected his pint before heading over, Bev moving her seat a little so he could drag one to join their small table.

"How you doing buddy?" Zeller asked with that annoying face of his.

"Just fine." Elias replied and there was a moment of awkward silence before Jimmy resumed whatever he had been saying before Elias had arrived. After a few minutes Elias tuned out of the apparently amusing conversation but his thoughts were interrupted when Bev leaned in and spoke quietly -

"How are you really? We've been worried. Adam was really worried. Only Brian has seen you and even he said you seemed really glum at work. Is everything ok?"

Elias narrowed his eyes at her. "I'm fine. I was upset because of the last time we spoke... I..." he grit his teeth. His expression was still hostile but he couldn't help but answer truthfully - "I thought you told Adam what I said and that he would be upset?"

"What you said?" Bev asked, looking confused. But then realisation dawned across her face. "About him being gay? Fuck, no Elias. Everyone has their foot in their mouth at some point... you more than most from what I can figure. And... there was no way we could tell Adam without him being upset, and we care a lot about not upsetting Adam, if we have a choice." She paused and looked him over appraisingly. "And I think you do too."

Elias clenched his jaw but nodded. "He's my closest friend." Elias admitted quietly.

"Yeah." Bev smirked.

"We spoke earlier and everything is fine... He wanted to stay of course, and catch up and do best friend things, but I insisted he go on his date and not let the poor fellow down." Elias puffed up as he spoke.

Bev nodded, smirk still in place, before thoughtfully mentioning - "Well, it seems to be going well with this *fella*. They had a date a couple of weeks ago? Adam seemed to like him, and then he called and they went out last weekend. So third date tonight is promising. It feels like the first time in ages that Adam has actually been serious about someone rather than just fucking around."

Elias was nodding but he could feel the colour draining from his face. Perhaps this was more serious a date than he had realised? Perhaps this man might become Adam's boyfriend and he would no longer need Elias as a friend after all?

Bev re-joined the conversation with Jimmy and Brian - some funny story from their honeymoon that he was sure Jimmy had likely told a million times but everyone was too polite to say. Strange people. And Elias downed his pint whilst watching the door.

He would just have one more and then go home, maybe call Adam in the morning to see how his date went and if he wanted to meet at Nadine's.

*

Four pints later, Elias was slightly slouched against Bev, or she was against him, he wasn't entirely sure.

"You know, you're alright Elias. I wasn't sure at first, because you truly seem like such an asshole. But… you're a nice asshole, sort of like Zeller."

"Hey!" Zeller interjected.

"I also resent that statement." Elias slurred.

Bev laughed. "Yeah, but in a different way to Brian. Different assholes."

"I should hope so." Jimmy chuckled and Bev groaned.

"Save me Elias from these idiots!" Bev laughed and threaded her arm through his.

"I… I need to use the bathroom." Elias excused himself and half stumbled through the bar.

He went straight to the empty cubicle and undid his trousers, surprised to find that his cock was only slightly hard, despite having clearly felt his usual urge. Perhaps it was the alcohol, because the physical touch of a woman - even if he wasn't really interested in Bev Katz that way - usually caused a reaction.

Despite not being fully hard, he still ached and Elias knew that it would only subside if he came. This was not something that was usually difficult, but as he took himself in hand and stroked, he found his cock was not as responsive as usual.

Stupid of him to stay and get drunk with Adam's friends. Perhaps he should have stayed home? Perhaps he should have asked Adam not to leave on his date?

He remembered the comfortable embrace and the scent of the man - so well matched to his beautiful face.

Elias bit his lip. His cock was hard now and in need of release. He quickened his strokes.

Perhaps he could have cooked Adam dinner or got takeaway? Spent time catching up over the days they had not spoken. Adam would have laughed - always a bright joyous sound. And if he had felt uncomfortable or dysphoric then maybe he would let Elias hold him close as they had earlier, as he'd wanted to many times before but had been unsure if it would be welcome - to reach out and give comfort to his friend. His good friend. Adam, his wonderful and close-

Elias grunted as he came, hot ropes of ejaculate hitting the cubicle door, remnants oozing over his fist. He put out his free hand to steady himself against the side of the cubicle, his knees weak and legs wobbly. He was surprised that Bev - who he didn't really even feel an attraction for - had had such an effect on him.

After he cleaned up, Elias went back to the table and grabbed his jacket.

"I'm going home. I'm tired." He told them. Brian was slumped against Jimmy's shoulder and Bev was nodding sleepily.

"I'm gonna call us a cab. You need a lift?" She asked.

He shook his head. "I live nearby." He turned to walk away but then was struck with a sudden thought of how Adam might want his friends to be treated. He turned back. "Thank you for a lovely evening." he mumbled at the table. Jimmy nodded and Bev shot him a thumbs up.

The walk in the cool air was at least a little sobering, and Elias stopped in to get a bag of chips from the kebab shop on the corner. He had eaten almost half of them in the open wrapped packaging when he got back to his home.

He was thankfully no longer hungry and slightly more sober when he dropped the remaining chips on the floor - surprised to see Adam sitting on his doorstep.

*

Adam hugged his arms around himself and Elias draped a blanket over his shoulders, before sitting next to him on the lumpy and uncomfortable sofa.

"You don't need to tell me anything." Elias told Adam, who was aware he had barely said two words since they got into the bedsit. "I can walk you home if you like?"

Adam shook his head and then took a deep breath before picking up the glass of water Elias had set on the dated coffee table in front of them. He felt like shit doing this, putting out his friend in this way but it had been the first place he'd thought to go. He didn't want to go home and be on his own. He hadn't planned to be alone tonight and... it was hard.

"Did he hurt you?" Elias asked, despite what he had previously said, and Adam smiled as he shook his head, defusing the imminent bluster.

"No. Nothing like that. I... I really liked him, I thought there was something there. And he knew everything, so it wasn't like I had anything to hide in any way. But..." Adam trailed off. The same thing, always the same thing and the reason why he preferred to just fuck instead of looking for something meaningful - he should have known better. "He decided there was too much baggage with me."

Adam pulled the blanket tighter around him and let out a shaky sigh.

"Well, that is most definitely his loss!" Elias declared with some overly emphatic hand waving that made clear his levels of inebriation.

"Maybe." Adam shrugged. It didn't matter. It never did. Just keep going. "I just, I didn't want to be alone tonight? I tried to call Bev..."

"She was drinking with me and Jimmy and his idiot husband. Do you want me to call her for you?" Elias reached for Adam's phone on the table. Adam wasn't sure how Elias would have ended up drinking with those three without him there, and it left him weirdly conflicted. Glad they were getting along but strange about the why. Was he interested in Bev? He wouldn't want things to get awkward if she turned him down, or a date didn't work out. It wasn't like he'd want to choose between them if it came to it. He shook the thoughts off.

"No. No, it's fine. I'm here now. I... I hope that's ok?"

"Of course." Elias nodded, again - emphatically. "I would offer you the bed but I don't want you to get offended thinking that I only offer it because I believe you to be more delicate than myself in anyway."

Adam blinked and then laughed. How could Elias still be sweet and thoughtful whilst also kind of insulting him?

"It's ok, I can take the couch. I'm butch enough for these lumps." Adam chuckled.

Elias frowned and bounced in his seat for a moment. "Yes, it is uncomfortable. Hmm… well, we can both fit in the bed."

Adam wasn't sure why he felt a small flutter in his chest and down to his stomach. The bed was definitely big enough for both of them, so neither *had* to endure the sofa. And it was nice and thoughtful of his friend to suggest it.

Adam nodded. "Okay."

Elias nodded in return and excused himself to the bathroom to prepare for bed. Adam ground his teeth together and wrung his hands as he sat on the sofa considering the evening's events. He could hear Elias in the tiny adjoining bathroom through paper thin walls - peeing, washing his hands, brushing his teeth.

Adam didn't have a toothbrush. The thought of bad breath shouldn't bother him as much as it weirdly did.

When Elias returned Adam went in and performed the same ritual, sans toothbrush and using his finger instead.

He took a few breaths. He hadn't shared a bed with anyone for a long time. Only to fuck and then kick out or leave. He didn't do sleepovers. He wasn't sure how he felt about being so physically close to someone. He swallowed. There wasn't a lot to be done now. He could always move to the sofa if he felt uncomfortable at all.

When Adam walked back into the room Elias was folding his clothes, stripped to only his boxers.

"I don't… I would give you pyjamas, but I don't ever wear…" Elias seemed very conscious of trying to make Adam comfortable so Adam smiled at the attempt and Elias went to the bed and turned down the covers. He couldn't deny that the view was more attractive than he might ever have guessed. Elias was nicely built and had a furred chest that was just the sort of thing Adam liked - on anyone else of course.

As Elias got into the bed Adam took off his shirt and jeans, leaving him in just a t-shirt and boxers. He was glad that Elias was facing away and not watching him, even more so when he got into the bed. He realised how nervous he was when he lay down next to his friend and was hit by the virile scent of the man, mixed with minty toothpaste. Rather than being uncomfortable it was strangely familiar and right.

Adam thought he should question that a little, but then sleep dragged him under.

6

Adam felt a comfortable weight against his back as he woke. It was odd, because he had moved his bed from against the wall months ago, so... His eyes flew open as he realised it wasn't the wall and this wasn't his bed, a heavy arm wrapped around him.

Maybe Elias felt him go completely rigid in his sudden anxiety because the man stirred and pulled him closer - the arm then shifting and a hand wandering down... It felt like the air was punched out of Adam's lungs and he was unable to move under the blind panic as Elias pressed his sizeable morning wood to Adam's ass, and his hand reached Adam's crotch. His own cock jumped at the sudden contact and he let out a whimper. His mind reeled - caught somewhere between being horrified and worried how this would affect their friendship and... wanting it? Surely just a result of the poor ending of his date the night before.

Adam shook the thought from his head. "No!" The word burst from him and he snatched Elias's hand from his crotch before it had chance to explore.

Elias jumped then and had scrambled out of the bed before either of them had chance to register the situation.

"Adam!" Elias seemed shocked to see him there. The man *had* been completely inebriated. "Adam, what, oh my... did we..." he looked completely panicked and Adam couldn't help the stab of hurt and feeling of rejection that he allowed himself to read into the moment.

"No. Nothing... I just slept here." He pulled the covers up around him, wanting to disappear and trying not to look at Elias. At his hard cock barely contained within his straining boxers, his compellingly greying fluffy chest, the warm depths of his eyes.

"I'm sorry. I didn't mean to-" Elias made a grabby, touchy motion with his hand. He looked flustered in a way Adam had never seen before and the clear distress seemed to override Adam's own as his panic waned.

"Hey, no harm done. It was a cold night." Adam forced a chuckle. "No wonder we ended up snuggled."

Elias nodded and clearly forced a smile. "Sorry..." he muttered again before excusing himself to the bathroom. Adam started to wonder if Elias actually meaningfully apologising was going to be a common occurrence from now on.

He sighed and pulled himself from the bed, hurriedly putting the rest of his clothes back on. Trying desperately to ignore how good it had felt to wake up with someone like that, even if it had freaked him out. He just wanted to meet someone where he could wake comfortably snuggled and not be freaked out.

Elias came back to the room, wearing a bathrobe and looking very sheepish.

"It's ok." Adam smiled. "Really."

Elias forced another smile and nodded. He looked so vulnerable and pained, in a way Adam hadn't really seen before. It made his heart ache, he wanted to comfort the man as much as he wanted to run away and hide.

Running away won out.

"I... I should get going. I need to get back to my place and shower and stuff." Adam pulled on his shoes. It was so weird to be making these excuses with Elias as he had done so many times with other guys. Leaving or asking them to leave in the middle of the night once the fun was done.

"Yes... I have things to do too. I'm very busy in fact." Elias countered in his usual self-important way and Adam smiled and nodded.

He grabbed his jacket and headed out of the bedsit.

*

Elias spent the evening alternating between pacing and sitting on the edge of his bed. He'd wrung his hands so much they were aching.

He looked at his phone and clenched his jaw. He should call Adam and ask if their plans for tomorrow were still ok. It was usually their movie night, but they hadn't spoken since Adam had stayed over and that was a week ago. Elias couldn't remember the last time they had gone so long without talking… Or at least before the whole Adam is gay stupidity. The thought caused a sharp pain in his chest.

Adam was such a good friend, he hated to think he had ruined everything. Maybe it might have been ok if he had answered one of the four phone calls Adam made to him the next two days, but he didn't have the nerve. He didn't know what to say. And now it was so much worse for having been left to fester and he couldn't just turn up at Adam's place as if nothing was wrong.

Even though Adam had said everything was fine when they had been in bed together.

But… he remembered *that* morning and shuddered.

He often woke painfully hard and would take himself in hand, even if just to hold it and try to quell the ache. But when he had reached for himself that morning, someone else's crotch was in the way.

His phone sounded then and he clicked open the text.

-Hey, hope you're ok. You haven't called me back. Are we still doing movies tomorrow?

Elias's palms were sweaty as he quickly fired back -

-Yes

Whilst he had the nerve. He threw the phone on the bed and wrung his hands a little more as if he could take back the accidental touching. His hand had definitely grazed over *something*. The memory sent butterflies through him. He hadn't put much thought before to what Adam had between his legs - it was none of his business after all. But he knew it must be very awkward for Adam and he had likely made it worse.

And it *was* worse! As the thought played on his mind and he felt the familiar ache. He whimpered as he pressed his hand to his hardening length.

*

"I'm so… urgh. Frustrated? Pent up?" Adam paced the living room and sighed. He was really trying to be polite, but things had seemed awkward since his sleep over at Elias's and he hadn't thought the man was going to show for movie night after a week of silence and his recent disappearance from Adam's life. In his head he had already made other plans and now he felt terrible about it either way.

When Elias *had* turned up there had only been a moment of awkwardness before they settled back into their usual easy ways. And he felt like shit for thinking about abandoning his friend, but… he was getting pretty desperate and if anything waking with Elias hadn't made it any easier.

Elias was sat on the sofa, flicking through the recordings on Adam's TiVo. "You know, you have over 40 recordings of this show - Judge Judy. Do you never actually watch them? What is the point of recording them."

Adam shook his head and rolled his eyes. "Are you even listening to me? I want to go out."

"For a walk?" Elias looked at him then, confused. "It's dark. Almost 8pm. Where would you walk to?"

"I don't want to walk Elias! I want to go clubbing." Adam dropped down onto the sofa next to his friend.

Elias raised a confused brow and looked at him. "It's movie night."

"I know." Adam near whined. "But… Ugh, I'm just. Look, you don't have to come with me. I don't know if it's really your scene. We can do movies another night?"

"I don't understand." Elias looked even more confused by the minute. Their plans were usually pretty solid - they had regular things they did - breakfast at Nadine's, brunch at Nadine's, drinks at the bar, drinks at the bar with Bev and Bedelia, movie night. But then shit had got a little weird and now tonight...

"It's the monthly fetish night at Vibes... it's not... I mean, I'm not especially into it. But I've had more luck picking up guys there than normal nights. They're more... adventurous." Adam tried to explain.

"I don't... you aren't a fetish." Elias's words took him aback a little and lodged a tight feeling of *something* in his chest.

"No I don't mean... I just. Elias, goddam it I want to get laid. It's been fucking months and I'm so sick of my hand I might divorce it." Adam flung said hand up, exasperated.

"Oh." Was Elias's only reply as realisation dawned. A clear realisation across his face, that tempered into a frown.

"I love movie night with you, I really do. But tonight... I'm horny and the opportunity is there so..." Adam shrugged.

The muscle in Elias's jaw worked as he clenched and unclenched it. He looked pained and like he might actually cry.

Fuck.

"It's nothing against you Elias. Maybe we can watch movies tomorrow?"

Elias shook his head and stood. "No, it's..." his words trailed off and he clenched his jaw again. He looked at Adam with sad and searching eyes.

"What? What is it?" Adam asked. It felt like there was something deeper at work than just missing movie night. Maybe Elias was feeling really lonely, Adam knew he did sometimes. Maybe this was as shitty a thing to do as he suspected, especially considering they hadn't talked in a week.

Adam felt conflicted and sighed. Before he could say anything else Elias grabbed hold of his hand. The gesture surprised him and he looked at tear brimmed eyes, desperation clear.

"Please don't go Adam."

"We can rearrange mov-"

"No. Adam, please." Elias's raised his voice and colour rose in his cheeks. "I don't want you to have sex with a stranger."

Adam frowned. "I'll be safe Elias, I always am. You don't need to lecture me on safe-"

"Adam." Elias said firmly, pulling Adam's hand to his chest. "Please... I don't. You can't have sex with someone else."

The phrasing confused Adam for a moment and then his own realisation dawned and he snatched his hand back.

"Elias... we're not... you can't." He sighed and closed his eyes, rubbing his brow.

"No of course." Elias's eyes were wide, like he was horrified at his own behaviour. "I..." He seemed like he was going to apologise but then resolve slipped into place. "Clearly, I didn't mean to suggest..." He stood and cleared his throat. "I should go, so you can..." he trailed off as though he couldn't say the words.

"Elias wait." Adam stood too and grabbed hold of Elias's wrist as he went to walk away.

"No. It's... I'm being..." He shook his head dismissively and looked down, though not attempting to pull from Adam's grasp. "I understand. I am not an easy person to be friends with."

"What? No, Elias that's not true, I just..." Adam searched for the words. He wasn't sure where all this was coming from or what it meant. He knew Elias held a weird jealousy for his other friends and seemed concerned that he was somehow replaceable. But that wasn't going to happen, no one could replace Elias. They had become so close and Elias was, weirdly, such a massive support to him. They had fun and were comfortable around each other. Elias did silly things to cheer him up on down days like getting coffee foam in his moustache and make like he didn't know, and Adam would laugh and feel tempted to swipe it away with his tongue just to see how the silly man would react. Elias was not replaceable.

"Please, I understand." Elias smiled sadly but still didn't look up. "I'm weird, I know. I'm not normal. I have an odd manner and I look hideous. And then this condition." He waved his free hand towards his crotch. "I am not easy."

"Elias that's not true." Adam felt a stab of something in his chest that he wanted to believe was pity. "You're my best friend."

"I wasn't always this way. I used to be very confident and well liked." Elias sobbed. "When I was a child. And even as I grew up, even after puberty and my problems started. Because at the time I didn't know they *were* problems, I thought that... I just thought that everyone was like this. In my twenties I realised that was not the case, as I grew close to someone and she rejected me - called me a freak and a pervert. And..." the words were almost lost in the sobs now and Adam could feel tears on his own cheeks too. "I know it's hard to understand, but-"

Adam choked out a laugh. "I understand Elias. It's the same... I never thought I was... I just thought everyone felt the same way as I did and it took me years to realise they didn't and address what was really wrong. And then it got so much worse, because then I knew why I was different and that it wasn't something I could change overnight. And all the feelings I had of being different and not quite right got worse. Just, so much worse once I realised what they were. I..."

He trailed off with a sob and looked down, realising he was somehow holding Elias's hand. Elias squeezed his fingers.

"I understand. I'm sorry it has been hard for you." Elias rumbled, his voice deep and warm

Adam let out an anguished laugh. It had been hard, so very fucking hard. But now he was the Adam he was meant to be and Elias still had to live with his condition. It made his heart ache. Because Elias was such a good friend.

He looked up from their hands and saw that Elias was looking up now. A sad sort of smile on his face. That warm and loving smile that seemed reserved only for Adam.

On impulse Adam reached up his free hand and cupped the side of Elias's face, smiling as Elias's eyes fluttered shut at the touch and he leaned into it. Adam drew his hand forward, Elias moving with it until their lips pressed together and Elias's eyes opened again - wide.

He pulled back but not out of Adam's grasp.

"Shit, Elias, I didn't mean to do that. I'm sorry. I'm horny and just… a fucking idiot." Adam was mortified. He wasn't even sure what the hell just happened. How did he just end up kissing Elias?

He didn't even want to think about how nice it had felt, how comfortable and easy.

Elias blustered but seemed unable to find the words, his face reddening and hands going to his crotch.

Shit!

How the fuck could he have done that to his best friend, knowing what he did. Knowing that that sort of physical contact from anyone might cause his condition to flare up.

Elias looked so embarrassed that Adam wanted to cry. He was about to apologise again when Elias snatched his jacket from the sofa and ran out of the flat.

"Elias!" Adam called but the man was already racing down the stairs and Adam wasn't sure he would appreciate Adam going after him in his current state. "Fuck. FUCK!"

He couldn't believe how much he had just fucked up his friendship. He shut the door and sat on the sofa, dropped his head into his hands and cried.

*

Elias paced the quiet bar. It was lunchtime and there weren't that many people there, and none of them were the person he was waiting for.

"Hey." Bev tapped him on the shoulder and he spun around.

"Being late is very rude." Elias told her.

"Hi to you too Elias." She smiled and then looked at her watch. "Besides, I'm pretty much dead on time, you got here early if anything."

"Yes, well. Hello Bev." He grumbled and allowed her to lead them to the bar and take a seat there. They ordered pints and a bowl of chips each, which would no doubt come out in baskets or on a plank of wood or something as equally ridiculous.

"So, what's up?" Bev asked.

"I wanted to talk about Adam."

"I figured." She smiled. "He called me after the other night."

Elias froze. He was trying his best to ignore everything that had happened with Adam recently. How he had touched Adam inappropriately. How he had made Adam feel so bad for him that he kissed Elias out of pity. The thought of him telling those things to Bev, especially the kiss, was upsetting.

"He crashed at yours after that shit date huh? What a fucker. He needs to find himself a nice guy. Know anyone?." She teased and hugged her arms around herself, fluttered her eyelashes. Very silly. But at least he was relieved to find Adam may not have told her everything.

"It is his birthday soon." Elias corrected gruffly, getting to the real point. He was going to make everything up to Adam and hope they could still be friends. And getting the right gift might be key to that.

Bev smirked. "So it is. Look, he hates surprise parties so don't even think abo-"

"No." Elias stopped her and shook his head. She could be very infuriating. "I want to get him a gift. And I seem to... I don't want it to upset him."

"What the hell did you want to get him?" Bev raised a wary brow but also grinned. Yes, *very* infuriating.

"A very nice scarf I have seen. He wears scarves a lot... But, I believe it is a woman's scarf." Elias lamented and sighed. "But... he would look so very nice in it. It is a blue-green, like the ocean. It would bring out his eyes..." he trailed off remembering how the thought had struck him as soon as he saw it. It was in a high end department store and would cost more money than he usually spent on gifts, but... it would suit Adam so beautifully.

"Holy fuck." Bev muttered. "You're such a pair of..." She trailed off and took a deep breath. "I think that sounds fine. More than fine. Adam loves scarves and he isn't exactly adverse to feminine things. I think it sounds like a great gift, I'm sure he'd love it." She smiled reassuringly and then added with a slight smirk. "Very thoughtful."

"Yes. Well, I am a thoughtful friend." Elias agreed, puffing up his chest.

Their chips arrived, thankfully in ceramic bowls, and they ate.

Bev spoke with her mouthful when she turned to him again - "You guys are pretty close now, huh?"

Elias froze again for a moment and slowly, ignoring the lack of table manners and hoping she knew no more than she had already let on replied - "Yes. I'm certainly his closest friend." Elias wondered if she would try and refute it, knowing how close her and Bedelia were with Adam. Not in the same way of course. No, the friendship he had with Adam was very different and not comparable and he needed to do everything he could not to spoil it, if he hadn't done so already.

"Elias, can I ask something personal? Feel free to, I don't know... not answer? But maybe don't throw one of your usual fits at least?" Bev asked tentatively.

Fit! As if he was prone to throwing fits. He narrowed his eyes at her but nodded anyway. She cleared her throat and looked like she was trying to find the right phrasing. It was very annoying having to wait for her to ask whatever it was.

"Are... are you gay, even just a little? Like, bi-curious or something?"

"No!" Elias's reply was immediate and indignant. He felt the colour rise in his cheeks at such a suggestion.

"Hey, no need to blow a gasket ok?" Bev held up her hands. "It's just... you and Adam, you're... really close. Just... in a very... *close* way."

"We are very good friends!" He blustered.

She nodded. "Yeah, I know. And hey. Seriously, don't go taking offense at that question. There's nothing wrong with being gay."

"Of course there isn't. I have no problem with gay people. But I am not gay! I asked Gabriel about it once, and he said that same sex attraction is very difficult and makes life very hard. Especially for someone like me." He stated emphatically.

"Um, yeah… what?" Bev looked at him like he had grown horns out of his head or something equally ridiculous.

"My brother. Gabriel. I asked him, when I was a teenager and girls made me… feel things." He cleared his throat. "And, also some of the boys. But Gabriel said it was just my condition and I was better off sticking to girls because it would be less complicated."

Bev nodded. "Right. Got it." She paused and chewed on her lower lip. "So… Elias, you do realise that… well, I mean I could be wrong. I'm usually not, but I could be…"

"What? You are so confounding, what are you talking about?"

"Well. I *could* be wrong, but… you do realise you *really* like Adam, right?"

"Of course, I like him! He's my best friend." Elias near shouted, beyond frustrated with the whole conversation. Why was she trying to lead him around in circles?

"No… you really *like* like him. Like… maybe more than a friend?" Bev's smile was sweet and reassuring and it made Elias suspicious.

"Is this a prank. Are you playing a joke on me?" We was suddenly terrified of how much Adam might have actually told her. He had no idea what on earth would make her come up with such a far-fetched idea.

"No." She dismissed it all casually with her hand. "Just a friendly observation."

"You are wrong." Elias laughed at the absurdity and tried to shrug it off. He looked at his watch and cleared his throat again. "Look at the time. I must be getting back to my desk."

Bev nodded and smiled. "Sure buddy. But look, um… if you are? It's ok. It's hard not to really *like* Adam when he lets you close like that." She smiled at him so warmly it was almost like they were friends.

He rolled his eyes and shook his head, waving a dismissive hand as he got down from the stool and left.

He walked slowly back to the office. Bev's words turning over annoyingly in his mind.

He did enjoy spending time with Adam. And Adam was very attractive, even for a man. And Elias had found men attractive before, but Gabriel knew best - women were put off by his condition, how much worse to be rejected by men as well. And Adam's lips were so soft and felt so nice against his own.

But no. Adam was his friend and he had never really had a good friend, so maybe this was just how good friendship felt. Such a good friend that he kissed Elias because he felt sorry for him. The pity hurt but the fact that Adam thought so well of him warmed him.

They were such good friends, they could talk about anything. Adam often told him about his dates. He told Elias often how he was rejected - laughing it off with sadness in his eyes. *Struck out again!* Elias wanted to hold him in those moments and make the sadness go away. He wanted to snuggle into him as they had awoken that one day. He wanted them to hold each other close and -

He touched fingers to his lips as he imagined Adam's pressed against his. What a soft sweetness it would be to kiss such beauty again. Elias shook his head and pushed away the silly thoughts. He was just finding having such a good friend confusing.

When he got to the office, Elias detoured to the bathroom, suddenly very hard.

7

"You did what?!" Bev's mouth was slack with astonishment and yet she was somehow still grinning. The way she had raised her voice above the evening hum of the bar made Adam wince.

"I'm a fucking idiot." Adam groaned and lowered his head into his hands, his elbows sticking to the surface of the soiled bar top. "And now we haven't talked in like, three weeks? And I miss him and I'm so sad I hurt him. I wish I could fix this. Just... rewind time and have it not all happen. Just go back and not fuck it all up."

Bev shook her head. "Ok, no - Bedelia help me out here." She looked past Adam to the other woman flanking him.

Bedelia took another sip of her wine then delicately placed the glass down in front of her. "Adam. Have you asked Elias how he feels about all this?"

"He feels fucking mortified!" Adam threw up his hands. "Haven't you been listening to me?"

"He told you this?" Bedelia quirked a brow.

"No." Adam begrudgingly admitted. "He didn't have to... He was so upset. I can't believe I kissed him."

"Oh! I can." Bev was grinning and something about that made Adam want to spill his drink on her, only she wasn't worth the wasted pint.

"Yes." Bedelia agreed and picked up her glass once more.

"The pair of you just…" Adam ran out of steam. He was going to lose his friendship with Elias, perhaps he already had, why wasn't anyone taking this seriously?

"Adam, on a scale of one to fucking miserable, where would you place yourself?" Bev asked but didn't wait for an answer as she continued. "Do you think you might have kissed him because you like him? As more than a friend?"

Adam's jaw tightened a moment before his chest did. "Don't be fucking ridiculous. We're just friends."

"Yeah, sure… Just friends that clearly dote on each other and are desperately sad when parted and *obviously* have a physical attraction." Bev counted the points off on her fingers.

"Well, you're just completely wrong. You could say that about me and any of my friends! Me and one of you two!" Adam countered.

Both he and Bev were caught off guard by the bark of laughter that erupted from Bedelia. "No. That's actually far from true, as you well know." She corrected in that school marm way she had.

Adam was shocked into silence by Bedelia's reaction, enough to consider whether it was in fact far from true. And maybe she was right, what he had with Elias *was* special. It was the closest friendship he'd ever had with a man, and it was close in a different way than any of his other friends. But then, Elias was so very different to all his other friends.

Adam waved a dismissive hand at them both. "You know what. It doesn't even matter what you're saying. We're just friends and… and even if you think that's not true, he's not gay."

"He likes you." Bedelia told him coolly. "As more than a friend, whether he realises it or not. I suspect not. It isn't easy for people who have had so few friends to-"

"Thank you Doctor." Adam cut her off. He didn't want to hear this, none of it was true. Elias was just upset because Adam had spoiled their friendship.

"Hey Elias."

Adam whipped around to Bev so quick he jarred his neck. She was talking on her phone and holding up a hand for him to remain silent.

"Yeah, it's Bev. So it's Adam's birthday in a few days, you know. And a few of us were going to go to the Fox and Hen for a few drinks to celebrate… Hey, no, that's not. Of course he wants you there. He asked me to organise everything and you're on his list. Of course you are you big lug! Yeah. Okay, well look, I know he's looking forward to seeing you….. Saturday at 7.30. Yeah, Fox and Hen. Cool, we'll see you there."

Bev made a show of pressing the red call end button and placing the phone back on the bar.

"For fucksake Bev!" Adam near shouted. "Why do you have to meddle?!"

"Because the pair of you, friends or whatever, will never sort your shit out if left to your own devices." She countered, still all smiles. Adam started to seriously consider spilling his drink on her after all.

*

"He's not coming." Adam muttered.

"What?" Bev looked indignant. "He text you? Called you?"

"No… I mean, he's not here yet and I still haven't heard from him since I, we… He's not going to show up."

"Shut up Towers. You're not a clairvoyant." Bev's grin returned and she brandished her pint at him. "You don't have clairvoyance enough to find the rebels' hidden fortress!" She accused and he laughed.

"You bastardised the line, but I can't argue with the sentiment." He necked the remnants of his second beer. "I need a piss."

He made his way through the crowd, several of which were at the pub to celebrate with him, and wished him well as he passed. By the time he got to the loo he was busting and rushed straight into a cubicle.

When he came out he was surprised to see Elias standing by the sinks, watching the door of his cubicle in anticipation. He stopped in his tracks at the sight.

"Hi." Elias started tentatively. "I was… washing my hands and you didn't see me. I thought I would wait for you." He sounded so small and meek it made Adam's chest hurt.

"Sorry, I really needed to pee. I didn't see you." Adam moved to the sinks, next to Elias, and began to wash his hands. "I didn't know you were here. I wasn't sure you'd…"

"Yes, I've been here for a while. But, you were busy with friends, I didn't want to interrupt."

"You're my friend Elias, it wouldn't be an interruption." Adam smiled and was relieved to receive a warm smile in return.

"I bought you a gift. It's with my jacket." Elias beamed.

"You didn't need to do that."

"Of course I do! What kind of person doesn't get a birthday gift for their best friend?" Elias bordered on indignant and it made Adam smile all the more. He really had missed that, as crazy as that was.

Elias started towards the door and Adam reached out and grabbed his arm to stop him. "Wait. Just… I wanted to say sorry. For everything and for things being awkward. I'm sorry about kissing you, I shouldn't have and I hope we can still be friends, because I miss you."

Adam tried not to ramble and cut himself short at just the facts despite wanting to say more, say anything not to lose Elias.

Elias smiled and nodded, patting Adam's hand on his arm. "Of course. You're my best friend Adam, I felt so bad that I made you kiss me. I-"

"Wait? No, Elias you didn't make me. It was my fault." Adam shook his head. "It doesn't matter now. As long as we can still be friends."

Elias nodded eagerly and started off again, Adam's hand still on his arm. Adam only realised and pulled it back as they got to the door - walking out arm in arm might give the wrong impression to everyone.

But especially to Chris - his date.

*

Elias felt warmed just having Adam walking next to him, having his friend there. He was so nervous and excited about his gift. He really hoped Bev was right and that Adam would like it.

He got to the table in the corner and turned to look at Adam, expecting him to be waiting for the gift but instead Adam was slipping into the corner seat and waiting for him to sit too.

"Oh! Don't you... I don't want to monopolise your time. You have many friends here." Elias felt a blush rising in his cheeks.

"Of which you are one Elias! I want to spend time with you."

Elias's chest swelled. "Well, yes. Of course. Who wouldn't. I am a very good friend."

"Absolutely." Adam agreed, beaming a wonderful smile at him.

"Oh! Here..." Elias pulled the gift wrapped packaged from his jacket pocket. "I had the shop lady wrap it as it saved fussing with buying paper, though I am sure I could have done a better job." Elias wanted to make that clear as he handed Adam the small package.

Adam's smile was still wide and dazzling. "This, you didn't need to, honestly. But thank you. Shall I open it now? My birthday isn't until tomorrow."

Elias's heart sank - torn. He really wanted to see Adam's face when he opened the gift if he liked it, but if he didn't...

"I'll open it now." Adam smiled, turning the package over in his hands and then carefully opening the delicate blue paper. It was all very feminine, and so Elias had opted at least for blue to make it seem a little less so.

Elias zoned out, a buzz of nerves in his ears.

"Oh, wow... Elias. It's..." Adam was grinning, pulling the chiffon over his fingers and Elias focused back in on him. He looked so happy, his eyes bright - made even brighter by the colours of the scarf as Elias knew they would be. "It's beautiful!" Adam donned it immediately, and it complemented perfectly the smart black shirt he was wearing with his jeans - open at the throat.

"*You* look beautiful." Elias said without thought or fear.

Adam smiled warmly, affection in his eyes that Elias had never seen from anyone before. A look he had always longed to see. He placed his hand palm up on the table and Adam reached across, placing his own smaller hand within his grasp. Elias closed his fingers over the top, never losing Adam's gaze.

"Adam, there you are." A deep voice interrupted the moment.

Adam's hand suddenly slipped from his and back across the table.

"Chris, hey. Sorry. This is my friend Elias, I mentioned him? He was just giving me a gift." Adam stroked a hand down the scarf.

"That's beautiful." Chris said, making the word feel suddenly so much cheaper to Elias. "Really brings out your eyes."

Elias grit his teeth and frowned, heart sinking. Who was this man to say such things to Adam?!

"Elias, this is Chris." Adam's cheeks were flushed and Chris held out a hand for him, Adam took it and was drawn to his feet.

"Mind if I steal Adam away for a bit Elias? When he said he wanted me to meet some friends I hadn't realised I wouldn't get any time with him myself this evening." Chris winked.

Elias was at a loss for words. Saying nothing, not moving, just taking in Adam's apologetic look followed by their backs as they headed towards the bar.

*

Elias sat back down with his third pint, not realising Bev had followed him until she slipped into the chair Adam had left empty over an hour earlier.

"Hey buddy. You good?" She smiled and it seemed more concern than pleasantry.

"Who is Chris?" He blurted the question before even thinking about it.

Bev winced. "Oh yeah, Chris. I guess Adam hasn't really mentioned… They went on a couple of dates, this is their third I think? Adam wasn't sure whether to invite him or not. I mean, he only told me about the guy yesterday! Said he didn't want to mention him until he knew if it was serious or not. I… guess it's serious." Bev shrugged and looked a little forlorn.

An expression Elias knew he reflected but could not even attempt to hide.

"Fuck. Fucking, fuck Adam. Fuck!" Bev muttered, startling Elias.

"What…"

"I just… Ugh. He's so fucking blind."

Elias frowned and Bev let out an exasperated sigh.

"He-" She started but then her eyes fixed on something or someone near the door to the pub and muttered "Oh shit."

She was up on her feet and heading into the small throng near the door. Four men had just come in and were making their way to the bar. Elias was still frowning trying to work out what had caused Bev to make a bee-line for Bedelia, Jimmy and Zeller when one of the newcomers drunkenly shouted just above the noise.

"Hey Sam. Sam! I see you. Fucking hiding in there. Is that your boyfriend?" The man chuckled and several of the crowd turned. Those with the man seemed a mixed bunch of embarrassed or amused. "I fucking see you SaMANtha, can't believe you didn't invite any of your work buddies for your birthday." Another cruel laugh.

The emphasis on the *man* in Samantha seemed curious, but Elias didn't have time to ponder as Zeller stepped forward, hands up in placation.

"Come on now Tony, you've clearly had enough to drink already, maybe you should call it a night."

Two of the others with this Tony seemed immediately uneasy and perhaps they agreed with Zeller.

"Well, actually we were on our way to get chips and then we pass by and look in the window and what do we see? The fucking lovely Samantha here, having her birthday celebration without all her work friends. Very rude, man. Fucking rude."

Elias frowned, confused, and looked over to Bev. She, Bedelia and Jimmy had moved to stand next to Adam, placing themselves between him and the action. But even so Elias could just see his mortified expression and red face on his friend.

Adam was upset. More than upset, he was anxious and deeply unhappy.

Elias was out of his chair before he even realised what he was doing. He stormed through the crowd like a bull in a china shop in his effort to get to Adam. To help him, to do whatever he needed to be happy and comfortable.

"Watch it mate." The angry Tony snarled at him, it was the only thing that made Elias realise he had almost knocked into him as he'd attempted to pass.

Elias spun on his heel and faced the man. They were of a height but Elias was bulkier and loomed over him. "You are very rude. Very!" Elias snapped as he pointed his finger in the man's face.

The man grabbed his finger and twisted it back until Elias was near cowed and crying out. Zeller was on the man's hand then, shouting as he tried to pry him off Elias.

And all the while Elias's blood boiled. He wasn't entirely surely what was happening, he just knew that this man was very rude and was upsetting Adam, and that did not sit well with him.

"Tony stop. Don't hurt him." Adam's voice rang through the crowd and the man loosened his grip enough for Elias to pull away. He found himself steadied by Zeller. And then Adam was suddenly at his side. "Elias, are you ok?"

"Fucking hell. Still such a slut. Can you believe it?" Tony was laughing to his friends, one of whom continued to look embarrassed, two others joined with low chuckles. "How many of these guys are you fucking, huh Samantha?"

The words were clearly directed at Adam but he didn't respond to them, he just continued to look at Elias. Determination clear and yet his eyes were full of an anguish that hurt Elias.

"I'm talking to you fucking slut." The man grabbed Adam's upper arm and pulled him roughly around.

The next moment was a blur. Elias wasn't even sure what happened until he hit the ground, his hands balled in Tony's shirt as he slammed him against the floor. He lifted him and slammed him down again, knocking the wind out of the man.

"You don't touch Adam."

He felt arms grabbing him, pulling him back until he was on his feet again and there was just noise and commotion around him.

Then the cool air hit him and he was standing in the street with Zeller. "Just go, get out of here Elias. We'll calm this shit down. Go before they call the fuzz."

Elias blinked at the man a couple of times. Zeller's face broke into a smile. "But, y'know, good work buddy." He slapped Elias on the back and then turned back to the bar. The door opened and closed on shouting and the bar bell ringing although last orders was a while off.

He wanted to go back in and make sure Adam was ok, but he knew he didn't need to and he didn't want to make things worse. It wasn't his place. Adam had Bev and Bedelia, Jimmy and Zeller… and Chris.

He thrust his hands into his trouser pockets and walked away.

*

Adam shifted nervously from foot to foot and checked his watch again, it was almost midnight. Maybe Elias was already in bed.

He was about to turn away from the door when it swung open, revealing Elias. He was in only his underwear and wiping his bleary eyes. At first

Adam thought it might be from sleep but then realised the red rimmed eyes were watery with tears.

"Adam?"

"You left your jacket." Adam held it out suddenly feeling foolish. "Can I... can I come in?"

Elias took the jacket and walked back into the bedsit, leaving the door open. Adam followed and shut it behind him.

"I'm sorry if I ruined your night." Elias said quietly, all the fight seemed to have been sucked from him and it made Adam ache.

"You didn't! I had a great time... well, until... Look, thanks for standing up for me with Tony. He's... I work with him." Adam paused for a moment but then decided very definitely to continue because it felt like something Elias should know. "I slept with him. A long time ago, we were fuck buddies for a while. I used to... I like sex and I never had much of a problem with finding sexual partners until I realised why some things made me so uncomfortable I wanted to vomit." He shook his head. "That's not important I guess... he didn't handle it well when I transitioned. He makes work pretty hellish sometimes." Adam shrugged.

"You don't need to tell me any of this." Elias said quietly.

"I do. I need to say thank you, but also... I just need to tell you... Um, thanks again, for the scarf. It's just so... I love it." Adam absentmindedly ran his fingers over the delicate material. "And for standing up for me... and for being my friend." Adam bit his lower lip and stepped closer to where Elias stood stock still, eyes cast down, in the centre of the room.

His breath caught as he reached out and took hold of Elias's hand, squeezing it in his. Grounding himself and trying to work out whether this was right. Whether Bev was right. How had he not realised these feelings before? Perhaps he hadn't wanted to, he sure as shit didn't want to lose their friendship. But...

His chest was tight, it ached and he knew his nerves would get the better of him if he hesitated.

He stepped in closer, so that he and Elias practically occupied the same space, his free hand cupping Elias's face as it had done that one time before. He guided him up and took in the forlorn deep brown eyes.

He leaned in and pressed a chaste kiss to Elias's lips.

"What about your date?" Elias asked when Adam moved back. The words seemed so full of pain that Adam hated himself.

"I told him I didn't think it was going to work out. I didn't want to hurt him by telling him the truth." Adam smiled.

"What truth?" Elias frowned.

Adam chuckled. "That he didn't have a chance because there was already someone I really care for and needed to go find immediately so I could do this-"

Adam pressed forward and kissed Elias again, sweet and gentle.

When Adam pulled back to look at him Elias looked confused.

"You mean me? Kiss me?" Elias asked.

Adam laughed. "Yes Elias. I needed to come and kiss you... to see if you would kiss me back."

Elias pulled him into another kiss, a little messy, wet and unrefined. And yet Adam loved it, it was everything of Elias.

Elias was panting when he pulled back from the kiss to draw breath.

"I... find this confusing." Elias mumbled.

"I didn't mean to-"

"Not the situation." Elias mumbled, looking unsure. "Not... um..."

"Because I'm a man?" Adam asked quiety, almost terrified of what the answer might be.

"Yes... No, because we are friends. And I've never... with a man before."

72

Adam breathed a sigh of relief. Part of him didn't even care if this didn't go anywhere now or ever, as long as if it did it wasn't because Elias thought of him as a woman.

"It doesn't matter." Adam shrugged. "You can just ignore labels and boxes, it never does any good to put people in them anyway. Just…" he shrugged. "Enjoy people."

Elias smiled and nodded. "I… would like to kiss you again."

Adam grinned and snaked his arms around Elias's neck, feeling so so very good when thick arms wrapped around his waist. Adam kissed him then, slow and deep as Elias opened to him. It spoke of Elias's inexperience, but also his willingness to be lead as Adam moved their mouths together until they found the perfect fit. And Elias moaned.

8

"Adam. It is rude not to answer the phone."

"Sorry. Maybe you are working? Please call me when you finish working."

*

"You didn't call me. Very rude Adam."

"I'm sorry, you can still call me please? You were gone and I'm worried."

"Adam. This is very bad that you are not calling me. I will call again tomorrow."

*

"Please Adam. I know I must have done something wrong. If you let me know what I did I can fix it. I'm sorry. Please."

*

"Adam?"

*

Adam played the scarf over his fingers. Light spilled across it as they sat in the cafe's window, catching the delicate variations in the blueness of it.

"I knew you'd like it." Bev smiled. "It was a thoughtful gift." She had a hopeful look on her face. But gentle rather than her usual eagerness for gossip. "So…" She looked down at the coffee in her hands. "You seen Chris again? He seemed nice."

Adam shook his head. Letting out a sigh before he even realised it. His chest felt heavy.

"Ok. That's it. What's going on Towers?" Bev demanded. "It's been two weeks since your birthday and I've seen nothing of you at all, neither has Bedelia. I thought at first you were holed up with the new boy, but we get vague texts putting us off and now you finally deign to have coffee with me and conversation is like pulling teeth. What is it?"

He shrugged, his eyes now firmly on his own coffee.

Bev's voice gentled a little. "Look, we're here for you, you know that right? Please. I'm worried. If you don't want to talk to me, may Bedelia, or even Elias? Is it a guy thing?"

Adam let out a little sob that he could no longer hold in. It was a desperate sound and threatened to pull more along with it, but he clamped his mouth shut and ignored the sting in his eyes.

"What's going on?" Bev repeated more instantly as she reached across the small table and took one of his hands. "Adam?"

He looked up at her and tried to not show how desperately sad he was.

"Elias… I fobbed Chris off and went to see Elias. And I fucked everything up."

Bev was silent for a moment, her brain clearly ticking over.

"Did… you guys sleep together?" She asked cautiously, clearly worried about upsetting him further.

"No… yes, almost. Not really?" He let out a long sigh and then breathed in a deep breath to replace it, regaining some composure. "We made out. It was late we were both tired, so we ended up in bed. Just kissing, touching… and then I completely freaked out."

Bev squeezed his hand. "What happened? Do you want to talk about it?"

"I just… I wasn't in a good place. I was upset running into fucking Tony and him being an asshole. And then the next thing I know we're kissing and we're in bed and Elias tried to drag my top off. And… it wasn't that he did anything wrong. I wanted that too, right up until the moment I didn't. I just had a sudden image of Tony doing the same thing, kissing me… kissing my…"

Adam withdrew his hand from Bev's to wrap both arms around himself. Even thinking about the memory made him feel more dysphoric. He'd never liked his chest being touched. Before he had shied from it or put up with it for the sake of whoever he was sleeping with. But once he had realised he needed to transition, it had become so much worse. Because he knew why he hated it and didn't want to have to do it again.

Even so, since top surgery, his chest was pretty numb and he might not ever recover more feeling than he had there. He was glad of it and had even enjoyed his chest being kissed or fondled since surgery. But that night, his brain had just decided it wasn't happening.

Adam shuddered at the memory and pulled his arms tighter.

"Oh fuck. Adam. I'm so sorry. Did Elias freak out?"

"No, I did." He clenched his jaw as he admitted it. "He was pulling at my top, and leaned in… he was k-kissing m-my… He was… and my top was stuck around my arms and I just freaked and pretty much fell out of the bed." Adam felt a silent tear roll down his cheek. "And I just grabbed my stuff and bolted."

More silence as Bev considered her words.

Adam curled as far in on himself as he could. "I'm such a fucking asshole."

"No honey, you're not… You, you like him is all."

"Well, of course I do." Adam snapped. "He's one of the closest friends I have and I should never have fucked it up, I just… The whole evening fucked with my brain, I should never have kissed him. And now I've ruined our friendship. This can never work between us, he'll just get scared off like the rest - too much baggage. Too difficult to deal with." He couldn't help the anger in his tone.

"Have you spoken to Elias about it? I can't believe he would think that. He's your friend, he knows you well enough to know what the deal is and not be scared off." Bev said gently, but then when Adam didn't reply after a few moments her tone became insistent. "Adam, have you even spoken to Elias at all?"

Adam's jaw was clenched so tight it ached. He forced himself to shake his head, trying not to take in what she said - as sensible as it was. Not even Elias would be ok with the anxiety and dysphoria, and what joe public might think of him being with a trans guy - not to even mention the anatomical...

"Dammit." Bev spat the word at no one in particular and reached for Adam's phone. "You haven't spoken to him in two weeks?"

Adam wasn't quick enough to unravel and snatch up his phone before she grabbed it. Really he should put some sort of lock on it, because then she was glaring at him.

"Adam. You have a million missed calls from him and a whole bunch of voicemails..." she flicked through different screens. "And texts."

He already knew of course. He'd even listened to some of the voicemails but they were all the same on a loop - Adam was rude and should call, Elias was sorry, Adam should call. They had started to wane, and in reality he knew the reason he was feeling so miserable was because he had stopped receiving anything altogether a couple of days earlier. Not that he had a right to feel that way, he knew.

"You have to call him. Adam, you have to... have you read these last messages? He's going to go to Denmark. What if he doesn't come back? It's not like he has much to keep him here." He'd rarely seen Bev look so concerned.

He huffed, suddenly and overwhelmingly annoyed by her interference. "It's not as easy as that. He's not gay and I'm a complete fuck up, so it isn't like it going to-"

"He's in love with you, Adam." Bev told him so gently, interrupting quietly rather than with her usual gusto, that he wondered at first what the joke was, but then he saw she was deadly serious. "And you-"

"Bev, just-"

"No. Shut the fuck up and listen to me. He's in love with *you*. With Adam. With whoever or whatever Adam is or isn't. He doesn't care he just wants Adam, it doesn't matter what you are or aren't, what genitalia you do or don't have. Don't you get that? Don't you understand that he loves you the way you deserve to be loved? The way you want to be loved? Look if you're not into him that's fine, you shouldn't go for it just because he feels it, not if you don't. But Adam if you do... and I *know* you fucking do, you have to go tell him."

Adam sat in stunned silence for a moment. A chill prickly all over his skin. He hated when Bev was right because she could be so insufferable about it. And he didn't even care this time.

He stood abruptly, knocking over his chair as he tried to pull his jacket off the back at the same time.

"I've got the damn furniture, just go!" Bev grinned as he turned to assess the damage he had caused. He looked back to her with a grateful smile and left.

*

Elias sat on his bed and looked at his empty suitcase on the floor. He hadn't decided whether he was going to visit home or whether he was leaving London altogether. He had no idea how many of his meagre possessions to pack. Might as well take everything?

It wasn't as if there was anything keeping him here. And yet, when he had said as much on his call to Gabriel, his brother had pointed out he had more now than when he had first arrived.

Perhaps to Gabriel it seemed so. He had a job now and a bedsit, a few people he might call acquaintances, maybe friends at a push. He had none of those things when he first arrived for his job interview at Crawford's.

All this was true. But then why did it feel like he actually had much much less than before?

An image of Adam smiling at him taunted him and he let out a choked sob.

His eyes darted to the shelf on the far wall. It held a few books and keepsakes -

A copy of *Neverwhere* Adam had bought him because he had never understood his references to the Angel of Islington - Elias thought it might be a gay bar. It turned out not to be and he had very much enjoyed the book.

A photo that Adam had taken of them both together at the bar for Saint Patrick's Day. They both looked ridiculous in hats shaped like pints of Guinness, but Adam's smile dazzled. He had printed it for Elias as a reminder of a fun night and Elias had found a nice, suitably green frame for it -the same colour as the green scarf Adam wore the first time they met.

The ticket stubs from the three times Adam had dragged him to the cinema on their movie nights - all complete nonsense but Adam seemed to laugh at the jokes.

Leaning against the wall was the nice new badminton racket Adam had bought him when he had joined the local sports centre to play. He said he wanted Elias to have a good racket so he could *whoop some ass!*

The thought tightened his chest. Adam could be rude and noisy and had worried Elias a great deal with his serial dating behaviour, but he was also kind and thoughtful. And he was Elias's only friend.

Had been.

Elias picked up his phone from beside him and turned it over in his hands. He should try to call or message again. He had clearly done something terribly wrong, the least he could do was apologise again before he left. Not that Adam would answer - he hadn't so far. Whatever it was, it must have been very hurtful and Elias only wished he knew how to fix it.

The moment had played over in his head so many times. Kissing and kissing and kissing. So nice and soft - Adam's scratchy stubble catching his own. It had been very nice, very enjoyable. And then he had been so clumsy trying to help Adam undress and getting his arms caught. But they had laughed, it had been silly. It had been so very wonderful.

And Adam was so beautiful and his skin was so soft that Elias had to lean in to kiss his chest. But then Adam was unhappy and sad and leaving.

The thoughts of the evening, as arousing as some of them should have been, did not stir him at all. Even so, every time he'd had to relieve himself since that night he had thought only of Adam whilst doing so - and cried uncontrollably.

How could he stay in London knowing he had hurt Adam so badly? He wouldn't want Adam to keep running into him and be upset.

He had said as much to Gabriel, who had gone silent on the phone for a moment before replying that it was a very selfless thing of Elias to do and asked if Elias was feeling quite alright. He of course pointed out that he was *not* feeling alright, as should be clear from an hour long conversation about hurting the person he cared most about in the whole world.

Gabriel had been very rude about asking him to stop crying down the phone.

Elias sniffed and typed in one last message, the words a little blurry through his misty eyes.

-I'm sorry, really very sorry for what I did. Whatever it was. I am leaving tomorrow so please don't be concerned about finding me in a bathroom.

He had only just punched the send button when his phone started ringing. Elias's hands shook so much when he saw Adam's name light up on his phone, that he nearly dropped it. He fumbled for a moment before managing to answer.

"Adam!"

"Damn, don't shout." A female voice replied and Elias was momentarily confused.

"Beverly?"

"Yeah, look - Adam accidentally left his phone. He's... he's a fucking idiot. Just don't move, okay?"

Elias frowned. "Don't move from where? That is a ridiculous request, what if I need to use the bathroom or make a drink, or answer the-"

He was interrupted by a hammering on the door to his bedsit.

"Please wait a moment." He told Bev and then stood, phone in hand and went to the door.

*

Adam was out of breath from near running halfway to Elias's place before he realised he hadn't picked up his phone. He had to hope Elias was there...

Oh god, what if he already left?

The thought filled Adam with anguish that spurred him on. Maybe that was why he hadn't been in touch the last couple of days? Maybe he was already in Denmark, in that middle of nowhere place he told Adam about that surely had no signal? Maybe Adam would never see Elias again?

The thought punched the air out of him and he had to stop for a moment to catch his breath. His legs felt like jelly from nerves rather than exertion and he wondered if he was even going to make it to Elias's place without having a panic attack.

*

Elias reached for the door handle when his phone rang again. Confused he looked down at the device in his palm, the line to Bev Katz on Adam's phone still open but now he had an incoming call from Gabriel.

He pressed the switch call message that flashed up.

"Gabriel?"

"Elias. This is difficult for me to say. I don't think you should come here tomorrow."

"What do you mean? It's very rude of you to change plans late notice like this brother." He admonished. "You wish me to come another day instead?"

"No Elias. Not at all. Don't come back."

A chill ran all over Elias and he felt tears immediately and uncomfortably prickling his eyes and nose. "What do you mean? I already booked the flight…"

"Ellen thinks, we both think, you are better there. Until the fight with your friend you were happier than you ever were here. Perhaps you can be friends again."

Elias was stunned. Such unfeeling cruelness from his own flesh and blood, to disallow him from returning. Maybe he would go anyway. He could get a taxi from the airport, he didn't need Gabriel.

There was another knock at the door, this time more tentative.

"Just a minute. I am clearly busy!" Elias blustered back at the door, before turning back to his phone. "I will get a taxi then." He had made up his mind.

"No Elias. You're not welcome… Not unless you are coming for a holiday with your… *friend*, to meet the family."

"What? What are you talking about Gabriel?" Elias was near shouting and so flustered he could feel his face burning.

Then there a quiet voice from the other side of the door took advantage of the lull in aggravation and said - "Elias, please open the door."

*

The door swung open and Elias looked exasperated and flustered.

"Oh, I'm sorry. I can come another time. I… I should have called." Adam mumbled, suddenly unsure. His confidence plummeted to the levels of some of those worst limbo days of his transition.

"Adam!" Elias looked confused or relieved, but still so aggravated by his call that he wasn't sure how to read the man. "I'm talking on the phone." The words were matter of fact, but perhaps meant as a brush off? Adam wasn't sure. "To Bev and then-"

"Bev? Why did she-"

"You left your phone. I tried to call you and she answered."

"You did?" Adam's features relaxed and brightened from the frown to a hopeful smile. Despite already being very red-faced, it seemed that Elias blushed then.

After a moment of silence Adam plucked the phone from Elias's fingers, encountering no resistance.

"Bev, I'm here. Thanks for earlier, I got this-"

"This is not Bev." A male voice returned in clipped English with an accent not dissimilar to Elias's.

"Oh, shit... I'm... Shit, sorry." Adam felt his face redden and his anxiety spike.

"You are Elias's friend? Adam?"

Adam had been about to hand the phone back when the question came. He nodded for a moment before remembering this was not a visual medium. "Yeah, yeah I'm Adam." Lord only knew what Elias had told other people about him after this last couple of weeks.

"Well, going on what Elias has said, I think you are both as bad as each other as to be completely ridiculous." Adam was too taken aback to reply as the man blustered on in a slightly more civilised manner than Elias usually managed. "Why can you not just kiss and go on a date and do such things instead of acting like idiot teenagers. It's very annoying. Tell Elias I said goodbye and he cannot come home until you are taking a holiday and visit us together."

The phone went dead and Adam wasn't at all sure what to make of it. He lowered his hand, staring at the phone, which showed the call end and then popped up with his own name. He put the phone back to his ear as he looked at Elias, utterly confused. Elias for his part looked too mortified to say anything.

"Bev?"

"How long was he going to keep me on damn hold? Adam! You're there. Great. I have your phone. You're not getting it back until you guys work it out. I want at least heavy petting. And I'm serious, next time I see you I want one or both of you to have hickeys. I'm not kidding Towers!"

The phone went dead again and Adam handed it back to Elias.

"What did they say?"

9

"I'm sorry. Whatever it was, please don't hate me." Elias's words were so sad they broke Adam's heart.

"Elias, I don't hate you. I… I could never hate you."

They were sat on the Elias's beat up sofa, both nursing hot cups of tea that were quickly cooling untouched.

After the phone calls had ended Elias explained the man was his brother Gabriel, which at least put a lot of that conversation into context. They had shifted from foot to foot, looking at each other shy and unsure until Elias had offered to make tea, claiming "It would be the British thing to do."

Adam had to agree, it *was* what they did in a crisis. Adam had laughed and Elias's delayed smile told him it was yet another occasion where it had not been meant as a joke, but he was happy to have amused Adam all the same.

They sat to drink and talk but minutes had passed before Elias had spoken first - a mumbled and heartfelt apology. Adam wanted to reach out and grab him into a hug.

"I didn't mean to hurt you. You did nothing wrong. I just got scared."

"I scared you?" Elias looked tearful at the thought.

"No. I…" Adam put his mug on the little table in front of him. "I was still upset from the party and I just didn't realise how upset I was."

Elias nodded his understanding. "And that is why you kissed me." He sounded unbearably sad.

"No, I kissed you because I wanted to. It was… after that, being… intimate. It was too much for that night after seeing Tony. But I shouldn't have ignored you, I should have talked to you. I'm a shit, I cut and run and I'm so sorry." Adam admitted.

Elias nodded though he seemed still thoughtfully sad. "I understand. I-"

Adam couldn't bear it any longer, this was too hard and there were only two options that he could really see - either he left and called it a day or…

He took Elias's mug and set that down too, before leaning in and pressing a quick, chaste kiss to Elias's lips.

Elias's startled and moved back on the sofa to look at him.

"If I kiss you back will you run away again?" He asked.

Adam felt a weight lift and laughed, again the delay before Elias joined in, though the look in his eyes still sought an answer.

"Not if you don't want me to." Adam replied. "I… I think I'd like to see where this goes, if you want to? If you think you can…" Adam searched for the words. "If you are ok being with a trans guy."

Elias remained silent for a moment. It seemed as though he deflated - all his usual bluster and bravado leaving him. He finally spoke quietly, and so obviously and completely honestly for what might have been the first time in at least his adult life, Adam was willing to bet -

"Adam, I don't have much experience." He swallowed hard as though he might choke on the truth, but he continued. "I have never been with a man, and only with two women and one of those I paid. I don't have many people I am close to but I'm starting to understand the difference between friendship and… And… I. What you are doesn't matter." Elias shrugged. "It's not as though I have so much experience that I know women any better than men. But I do know, it is the connection that matters. I don't want to just have sex with someone, I want to be connected to them. If I have that connection, what does it matter if they are male or female?" He considered for a moment and some of his bluster returned, he jabbed a finger at no one in particular as he pointed out "Do you know how many people wish for a connection and don't find it? Or ignore it because it is not with the idea of a person they had in their head. Idiots."

Adam couldn't help but break into a smile. "Are you connected with me?" he asked, a teasing note to his question in an attempt to hide his anxiety over the answer.

"Yes." Elias replied immediately, then admonished - "But you don't make it easy! You are incredibly infuriating at times. Running and hiding is a very bad way to deal with things. I would never do such a thing." Adam continued to smile as Elias puffed out his chest. "In future perhaps rather than run away you can hide with me, let me help you. You can talk to me or I can just hold you. Whatever you need… as long as you don't run away." The last was put gently and it made Adam's heart ache.

"I'm sorry about the last couple of weeks, sorry I hurt you… Would you give me another chance? To pick up where we left off?"

Elias hesitated for a moment and then reached and took Adam's hand. He looked so small and scared, his inexperience feeling so delicate next to Adam's, which he'd freely admit bordered on promiscuity.

"I… I liked kissing you. Your lips, your chest. I liked it. I would like to kiss you more." Elias's words were certain even though there was a fear of rejection clear in his expression.

Adam smiled and stood, pulling Elias up with him and leading him to the side of the bed.

"I'd really like that." Adam agreed before letting go of Elias's hands to remove his t-shirt. He felt anxious for a moment, terrified that the dysphoria and previous thoughts would return, but he pulled the focus away by reaching for Elias's polo shirt and pulling it up and over the man's head.

"You're so beautiful Elias." Adam sighed, running his hands up into the hair decorating the broad planes of Elias's chest.

"I've been told so, many times." Elias's automatic reaction made Adam smile. He knew it probably wasn't true, but he wished it was. Elias deserved to be told every day that he was beautiful.

Adam ran his hands up Elias's chest, feeling the man shudder as they reached his shoulders and then snaked them around his neck. A moment later they were kissing again, soft and sweet. Elias moved his tongue in a way he had learned Adam liked the last time, and the kiss was everything. Firm against his own, not too wet, and most of all well remembered.

Their kiss deepened as Elias's arms closed around him. Their bodies pressed together, Adam groaned at the feel of Elias's hefty cock pushed against his hip.

Adam broke this kiss and looked at Elias. He had just been about to ask the man to fuck him, but the look in his eyes - tender and soft - made Adam grab for different words. "Elias... would you... I'd like you to make love to me."

Elias practically vibrated in his arms, he looked flustered and aroused and unsure, yet determinedly certain at the same time. He didn't seem to have the vocabulary to answer so Adam saved him by kissing him again.

They kissed and rut against each other, moans mixing in the otherwise soundless room. Perhaps that increased Elias's confidence, because another moan from Adam had the man lifting him off his feet and turning them to the bed. Elias broke the kiss long enough to lower them both down to the mattress.

Then he nuzzled into Adam's neck, drawing another moan as Adam opened his legs and let Elias settle between them. When they started kissing again Elias was thrusting against him, no doubt trying to get some relief on his aching cock.

A sudden thought struck Adam, that had this moment not been so intense, might have made him laugh. He had not wanted for sexual partners as a woman, he loved sex. He had a harder time getting laid since transitioning but got by. Something he missed any time something even resembling a relationship ended, was the loss of regular and easy sex. The thought of letting Elias fuck him every time his condition flared up made Adam whimper.

It made him want to feel Elias all the more.

"Wait." Adam broke the kiss and pushed Elias back gently with his hands on his chest. "I... I guess we should talk about... anatomy? I don't want to spring any surprises on you." Adam forced the words past his sudden nerves.

"You don't have to. I'm sure I can work out what goes where." There was a slight hint of annoyance at a possible accusation of the contrary which made Adam smile.

"No. I meant… It's not… I'm not like a cis man. My penis it's…"

"I've never been with men, so I wouldn't know."

"You know your own cock… and it's… Elias, you're *very* well endowed." That much was so obvious it might as well have its own postcode. "I'm not. I haven't…"

"Adam. Would it be easier for you to just show me? I believe I am more than ready to see you naked." Elias's hard cock still pressed to Adam's thigh confirmed the truth of his breathy words.

"Ok…" He mumbled and began to undo his trousers. "I… the surgery I had. I haven't… I had a clitoral release." he was fumbling with the zip now, shaking, and felt comforted when Elias's big hands closed over his and helped guide them down. "Testosterone gives you some growth and I didn't… lower surgery is very personal, the way people choose what's right for them and why. And I…" Elias had moved back and was pulling his trousers and underwear slowly down for him, sliding them over his hips as Adam lifted them and discarding them once they were off completely.

Adam felt very aware of the stp-come-prosthetic that was still strapped to him. Elias frowned for a moment as he appeared to be working out what he was seeing. Adam, heart racing, helped by lifting his hips again and pulling down the harness and packer. Elias's eyes went wide then with realisation and he took over from Adam, ever so gently pulling that part of Adam away.

Elias hesitated at the end of the bed and then must have decided that it was unfair to let Adam suffer nudity alone like this. He quickly - with the skill of someone who dropped his trousers many many times - divested his remaining clothes. Adam looked down the bed and bit his lip at the sight of Elias's form. Strong and muscular under his deceptive clothing, his cock larger than Adam had even thought - thick and gorgeous, and leaking copiously.

Elias climbed back toward him then, sitting between his legs. Adam threw a hand over his eyes at the thought of being scrutinised. He'd been with enough guys since his surgery and hadn't given a shit what they thought, but he cared what Elias thought. He cared...

"Your penis is very small." Elias said bluntly. Adam clenched his jaw and stole a glance at Elias to read his expression and found it a mixture of things, most notably lust. Adam's confidence spiked back toward his usual bedroom mode, self-consciousness receding.

"Mmhmm, but you make it so fucking hard." Elias's cock jumped and Adam smiled. "Does making me hard turn you on?"

Elias stumbled over his words before finally just nodding in response, his cheeks flushed. He seemed like he was going to lean in and kiss Adam again, but instead he looked back down at Adam's cock.

"They made you a little penis?" Elias asked, a mixture of curiosity and lust.

"Sort of..." Adam replied, snaking a hand down his body and between his legs. He took hold of his small member and began to stroke it slowly. Elias's hand moved to his own erection and copied the action, unconsciously it seemed. Elias watched the movement of Adam's deft fingers over his cock with unguarded lust. "I was lucky - I had a good amount of growth from the hormones, the surgery just freed it up."

"You don't have testicles" Elias voiced his observation aloud as his eyes moved down, followed by his free hand, lightly touching. It made Adam wonder exactly how much Elias knew about testicular implant options. But then-

Adam gasped as gentle fingers ran alongside his own and then down. And down. Adam closed his eyes, enjoying the sensation and wanting more, and then -

"Oh!" Elias's fingers found his front hole. "But..." Adam opened his eyes and could see another moment of truth about to happen and enjoyed the burn on Elias's cheeks the preceded it. "I looked up... before. About Anal sex? In case you wanted to or, you could... maybe try...But, do you..." He seemed to table all the conflicting thoughts in his head before letting out a settling breath. "What do you like Adam? What shall I do?"

Adam smiled and felt his heart melt. So many times both before and since his transition, he'd never come close to hearing those words. So often, as much as he loved sex, he just felt like little more than a human-shaped masturbatory aid to a lot of guys.

"I… I like to be penetrated. Um… either way is fine. I don't…" He felt his own cheeks burn as he spoke. He cleared his throat and tried to muster sexy, confident Adam again. "Do you have condoms and lube?"

Elias shook his head.

"It's ok. I just… I want you inside me, but… I need. Even with…" Adam stumbled over his phrasing. "I don't produce as much, um… I'm not so wet now, with the hormone therapy. So, even with the… front… I…"

Elias nodded his understanding but said nothing.

"I do have condoms, in my wallet though." Adam added. "They're a lubricated brand, so we could… we could try… Not anal, the… other…"

Elias nodded again, his eyes slightly wider. Elias's fingers were gone from him then as he reached down and fished Adam's wallet from his pocket before dropping the jeans again. He opened it and took out the three adjoined condom packets and ripped open the first. Adam watched the actions intently and wondered if the condom was even going to fit Elias. It might be a bit of a squeeze, but the man looked as desperately in need of this as he was. They'd have to buy larger for next time… the thought stole his breath. *Next time.*

Once rolled on with some wincing, Elias moved up the bed once more and settled between Adam's legs, their differently sized lengths pushed together. Elias leaned in and kissed him then, long and slow and improving with every moment. His hips gave the occasional and involuntary thrust against Adam, which made them both moan.

"Oh god, I want you so bad." Adam muttered as Elias moved down and their hips were no longer pushed together. The loss made him shudder, no less than when Elias then laid kisses over his chest. Just enough sensitivity remained to feel the lightness of the touch, the delicate teasing of one of his nipples.

A slight moment before the touch became too much for Adam, Elias moved again, further down. Halting when he came to the hair that trailed from just below Adam's belly button to his crotch. Elias nuzzled into it and followed the path ever downward.

Adam was panting as hard as his heart was racing.

He groaned and arched off the bed as Elias took him into his mouth. Again delicate and tender as lips and tongue wrapped around him and Elias drew back, sucking softly.

"Oh fuck!" Adam cried as he near levitated from the bed. He settled back but couldn't help but jerk every time Elias repeated the action. One of Elias's hands reached up and kneaded at his chest, pinched his nipple. Adam was surprised at how good it felt, but then Elias did make everything that little bit better.

Another long suck and Adam whimpered. He felt a little moisture gathering between his legs - his body trying hard to respond to the arousal he felt.

"You're making me wet." He moaned, both hands snaking down into Elias's hair. He might have been tempted to push the man further down but he was already going. A last swirl of his tongue and then it moved lower, trailing down until it reached Adam's front hole. Elias repeated the swirling action, wet and messy as he nuzzled at Adam's flesh. And then he pushed his tongue inside Adam and he keened again.

"How can you be such a natural at this?" Adam marvelled as Elias fucked his tongue into him, the whole area becoming all the more wet for it. "Oh fuck. Elias, please. I want you to... I need..."

He gripped his hands in Elias's hair and then moved them to the hulking shoulders which he grabbed and tried to manoeuvre. Elias seemed lost in his own pleasure for a moment and then allowed Adam to guide him back up. Adam smiled and wiped the moisture from Elias's moustache before pulling him down to mutter next to his ear. "Please Elias."

Elias pulled back and frowned. "I don't want to hurt you."

"We'll go slow." Adam agreed. "I'll be ok."

Elias bit his lower lip but nodded and Adam snaked a hand between them, savouring the feel of Elias's cock on his palm before guiding him between his legs. Elias was panting and red by the time his cock pushed against Adam's entrance.

"Are you ok?" Adam was concerned.

"I… don't want to cum too soon." Elias owned.

Adam pulled him down into a kiss and let his legs spread wider, hands up around Elias urging him to move forward. Elias did so then, slowly. His cockhead slipping inside to both of their groans. He drew back a fraction before pushing in again.

In truth Adam was wetter than he had been naturally in a long time, but still it stretched and burned in a way that was near unpleasant, but no worse than rough sex and it eased quickly. "Keep going." he muttered against Elias's mouth and wrapped his legs up around the man, trying to pull him deeper.

Elias continued slowly, each move forward a burn of pain and then the pleasure of fullness. Once Elias bottomed out he stilled, panting and squeezing his eyes shut.

"It's ok if you cum, Elias. I want you to. I want to feel you inside me." Adam clenched his muscles around Elias, drawing a gasp from the man.

Elias took a breath and nuzzled into Adam's neck, before he moved again. Shallow, slow thrusts at first.

The burn eased off, replaced by the sensation of being so filled, and his own cock captive between the friction of him and Elias. The only thing that could possibly make the moment better was if he had a butt plug too - the exquisite tightness that would add… Maybe next time. Next time…

"Fuck me." Adam groaned at the thought and squeezed his thighs tight around Elias. Elias repositioned himself slightly for better support and then began to fuck into Adam. Hard and fast and oh so deep. Adam's cock benefited from each slide of Elias's body until Adam was a writhing mess beneath him. Whimpering and moaning as his orgasm built and built. "I'm so… so close." Adam said.

Perhaps that was too much because then Elias stiffened and groaned, the wetness of tears apparent against Adam's neck as the man shuddered and then followed with a few erratic thrusts as he spilled himself inside Adam. As Elias continued his gentle thrusts through the aftershocks of his orgasm, Adam squeezed a hand between them and worked his own cock for a few short moments before he too was cumming hard. Elias cried out as his now, undoubtedly sensitive cock, was gripped by Adam's inner muscles.

Elias all but collapsed on top of Adam then, and they breathed together. Neither that fussed about moving and Adam quite content for Elias to soften within him.

*

Elias woke feeling bone tired and sated. It took him a moment to remember the previous night of exploration and sex and tender touches and undoubtedly the best blow job in the world once he had become hard again after the first sex.

Adam.

His eyes sprang open and he half expected the man to have fled again, but there he was. Curled into the pillow in front of him and breathing softly. The chiffon scarf he had gifted Adam was draped over the edge of the bed and Elias's cock twitched at the memory of sliding the material over Adam's soft skin a few hours earlier. He shifted over until he could wrap an arm around Adam and bury his face into soft, curled locks of hair.

Adam was so beautiful. Like one of those Grecian statues in the museum, that had a slender and toned body and small penis. His skin was smooth and pale like warm marble. Perhaps it was the lack of sleep, but for a moment Elias wondered if perhaps Adam might be a god.

The sex had been amazing, it had felt right, and very Adam. And Elias was happy to admit that he had taken more than a little liking to Adam's cock. The way it had fit in his mouth had been delightful and he wanted the chance to make Adam cum that way some time, as he had in Adam's mouth around 3am.

Maybe later that day if Adam liked? It surely sounded to Elias like a better option than being on a plane to Denmark after all.

10

Six Months Later

"I'm sorry." Elias looked up, that damn worried look on his face. Sometimes Adam actually wished he didn't apologise quite so much these days, especially when he had flare ups beyond his control. But shit, if it didn't undo him every damn time!

"It's ok baby." Adam smiled and stroked a hand down Elias's cheek, feeling the slight stubble and licking his lips as he imagined that same stubble shortly rubbing against his skin. "I wasn't exactly having a good time anyway." Adam chuckled.

Elias smiled and shook his head. "No." He agreed and Adam's lips twitched into a smirk. The taxi ride back to his flat from the perfunctory leaving do his job had thrown him, felt unbearably long.

In truth, he'd been glad for the excuse to leave the depressing affair. It was most definitely a personification of his time at the place. Years he had worked there and yet he was not going to miss a moment of it. It helped that the new job he was starting in a fortnight was so much better. Better position, better opportunity, better money, better colleagues. Better location... though the fact that it was near to Crawford's and would allow Adam to meet Elias for lunch or after work whenever they liked was not a factor. Just a bonus.

"I was glad to leave. I have more important things to take care of than trying to assuage the guilt of assholes who treated me like shit for years." Adam snuggled closer to Elias as he said it. He desperately wanted to slip his hand between Elias's legs and feel the hardness he knew was there, but he didn't want to risk Elias cumming in the back of the cab.

They both exercised the most admirable restraint until they were out of the cab...

And then he was on Elias, smiling into the kiss when Elias instantly opened to him and his arms pulled him up. Adam wondered whether the cabbie was still watching, as Elias's hands moved down and grabbed Adam's thighs. They moved together until Adam's legs were wrapped around Elias's waist and they clung together as Elias slowly made his way up the stairs to Adam's apartment whilst not breaking the kiss - moustache scratching against him.

Getting through the front door and into the bedroom seemed like a blur as Elias dropped Adam to the bed and they instantly began tearing off their clothes.

Adam loved this. Loved it when he was in a position to take care of Elias when he needed him. The thought of working so close flashed up in his mind again and he knew he'd have to be careful not to get either of them fired with lunchtime shenanigans! Elias did so much for him, gave him more support just by being Elias than Adam could ever explain - it felt good to return as much of that as he could.

"How... I'm very close Adam. How do you..." Elias's face was as red as his dripping cockhead.

Adam stifled a groan at the thought. He knew Elias meant that prep time was an issue. He knew Adam enjoyed anal as much as anything else, but sometimes there were practicalities. And although Adam could feel the slight moisture gathering that Elias managed to draw from him, he dropped onto his front and raised his ass.

"Surprise." He laughed and enjoyed the shocked silence, looking back over his shoulder at a stunned Elias. "I knew I wanted to take you tonight either way and didn't want to wait so..."

Elias's Adam's apple bobbed as he gulped at the sight of one of Adam's favourite plugs nestled between his cheeks.

"Adam..." Elias managed before scrambling to, what he referred to as *Adam's sex drawer* in the bedside cabinet.

Adam played with the end of the plug whilst he watched Elias don a condom and lube up in record time. In truth having the plug in and knowing the surprise that awaited Elias was the only thing that had made the evening bearable for Adam. He felt rewarded by the enthusiasm his surprise garnered.

Elias didn't seem to genuinely have a preference in how they had sex, though he clearly enjoyed giving Adam blow jobs, probably more than anything else. And Adam was so happy about that. It spoke volumes of who Elias was that he got as much pleasure from sucking Adam's cock as he did, when the man literally needed have his own cock seen to as a medical imperative.

Elias moved behind him on the bed, kneeling a little further off so that he could place a gentle kiss on Adam's right ass cheek before starting to work the plug in and out and then removing it all together whilst Adam writhed and groaned. Elias had been a ridiculously quick study. The man was built for fucking and he soon surpassed his master... perhaps in part thanks to google, Adam was sure.

Adam moaned as the plug slipped out and he felt Elias move forward and then the press at his fluttering hole. Thoroughly lubed, Elias pushed in slow but firm, sinking all the way to his balls as they both groaned.

"Fuck." Adam muttered, collapsing forward on his shoulders a little and snaking a hand between his legs to touch his own hard cock.

Elias grunted and took hold of Adam's hips.

"Hard Elias... Please." Adam begged. Before he'd finished his plea Elias was pounding into his ass and grunting all the more.

He knew Elias wouldn't last long, but it didn't matter. He just wanted to feel him, and the night was far from over.

Less than three minutes of furious thrusting, that had Adam gasping and drooling against the pillow, Elias shuddered and slowed, gently thrusting through his orgasm as he let out a deep and guttural groan. He draped himself over Adam's back and they panted together for a short while.

Adam was glad Elias had finally stopped apologising when he believed he had cum too soon. The fact was it really didn't bother Adam, and Elias's refractory period was astounding, so Adam would definitely take the trade off. Having sex several times in a night was something he was never going to get tired of.

As their breathing slowed and Elias started to soften a little he pulled out. Adam could hear the peel and knotting of the condom a moment before it hit the waste bin in the corner of the room.

Then large hands were on his hips again, another kiss to his ass cheek before Elias expertly flipped him over and licked his lips, looking down at Adam with an insatiable hunger. Within a moment Elias had dropped to the bed between Adam's legs, arms looped around his thighs as he drew Adam's hard cock into his mouth. Adam moaned and let his head drop back as Elias went to work on him. His ass still twitching and dampness gathering between his legs as Elias sucked and licked and nuzzled in a way Adam had become blissfully accustomed to and yet would never tire of.

Hours it felt like. Hours and hours of bliss delivered by Elias's mouth… and then his fingers. Adam gasped as Elias slid two fingers into his front hole and immediately found the spongy spot he had become well acquainted with over the months. Adam panted and writhed and tried to fuck up into Elias's mouth and onto his fingers simultaneously as his boyfriend undid him so fucking beautifully.

"Oh fuck… Elias I… I love your hands and your mouth and your cock… Oh… Fuuuuuck…" Adam shuddered as his orgasm ripped through him. "I love you Elias." He cried out.

*

The sun was up, and Elias had been awake for a while, just holding Adam and running soft fingers over Adam's naked back. He felt Adam stir and knew he had been awake for some time but was tired and too comfortable to move. When Adam stretched against him and said good morning Elias had to speak up.

"Adam… I want to ask a question."

Elias broached the topic gently. He knew that a lot of things could be said in the heat of a moment. Whether in anger or…

Adam frowned up at him where his head lay on Elias's chest. Elias couldn't blame the reaction. The last time he had used this same approach, a few months ago, Adam had been upset.

On that occasion he had asked Adam if he was happy with the size of his penis. Adam had got upset and accused Elias of wanting someone more well-endowed, which was not the case. He had only been curious as he had read that some trans men decide to have further lower surgery - google was not always the friend he thought it was!

Once Adam had been reassured that his penis was perfect because it was attached to Adam and no penis, bigger or smaller, would be as perfect if it wasn't attached to Adam, they made up and he pegged Elias for the first time with a strap-on.

Elias's cock twitched at the memory. He wasn't sure what he'd done to deserve someone as amazing as Adam. Adam was not only his best friend, he had also opened a whole sexual world to him after decades of knowing only the increasingly pleasureless regimen of his own hand.

Adam was looking at him expectantly, his brow furrowing more with each passing moment. So Elias forced out the words.

"Did you mean it? When you said you love me?"

Adam's face was red within seconds, a blush that reached the tips of his ears. Elias had never seen anything quite like it. It made his throat ache and his eyes sting.

"Um… yeah, I guess I did." Adam looked like a rabbit in the headlights for a moment before hiding his face in Elias's chest and mumbling against his skin. Elias could just make out the muffled "I'm in love with you."

Elias swallowed hard and his chest swelled.

"I'm in love with you too." Elias blurted and then sucked in a breath, determined not to let out a sob.

"I know." Adam giggled against him. "It's not a secret."

*

"Have you met my boyfriend?" Elias was beaming with pride as he asked one of his colleagues. They were stood in the sun on Jack Crawford's lawn for a company barbeque. The first they had attended together since the day Adam had tried to help Elias in the bathroom and had left in tears.

Such a difference time could make.

"Yes, this is my boyfriend Adam. He's a very talented journalist." Elias had continued before he'd received an answer, his arm tightening around Adam's waist.

Adam couldn't help but grin. Part of him found it cringeworthy, but that part was shouted down by the elation he felt at feeling so loved, so publicly loved by someone who was proud to call him his boyfriend. The thought brought a blush to his cheeks.

In the weeks since they had first confessed their love to each other Adam had not tired of hearing it several times a day. Sometimes said in passing, sometimes whispered against his skin. It had become a casual part of their everyday vocabulary, and Adam knew he was never going to tire of it.

"Adam, Elias!" Bev called out from the other side of the garden and Adam excused himself, leaving Elias talking with a lady from the marketing department. He seemed to be making friends at work more now and it certainly helped that since that night with Tony, Zeller had his back. In fact, they had become… well, not friends, but Elias tolerated him and Zeller found that endlessly amusing.

"Hey Bev." Adam smiled and Bev gave him the same knowing grin she'd been giving him for months. The grin that said - *I knew you'd be deliriously happy, thank fuck for my meddling.*

"You crazy kids having fun?" She asked, linking her arm with his and walking towards the makeshift bar.

"Oh you know, just being paraded around like some sort of trophy boyfriend." Adam grinned even through the faux annoyance in his tone.

Bev chuckled. "Oh, you love it!"

Adam laughed. "I kinda do. But don't tell Elias I said that. I've already had to get him to take it down from an 10 to a 4."

"That's a 4?!" Bev shook her head with mock concern. "That poor fella's got it bad."

"Yeah. Turns out, I'm pretty irresistible, to the right guy."

Adam didn't realise he was staring back over at Elias, arguably dreamily, until Bev poked him in the ribs and handed him a cool can of beer.

"Can I just... I love that you are so happy." She shook her head and chuckled - "I just can't believe it, y'know? When I think about how you guys first met, the first couple of times and just... I don't know. Imagine someone telling back at that last party of Jack's you went to you'd end up marrying that man-"

"What?!" Adam interrupted his smile dropped as his blush rose. "We... we're not getting married."

Bev laughed. "Yeah, like how you guys didn't *like* each other like *that*. And how you *totally weren't* in love. I mean, come on Adam... who are you going to believe? Me or your own denial?"

Adam laughed and shook his head. "It isn't happening."

"Maybe not today, maybe not tomorrow, but... well you know how it goes. Look, just make sure I'm best man or whatever when the time comes, I have some stellar ideas for your stag do."

*

Adam lost track of Elias after a short while, but couldn't help but be really happy at how well he was getting on with his colleagues. He was content to leave the man to his own devices, as nice as it had been to be paraded around, as Bev suggested. An hour of it had been quite enough. He was pretty sure he was proudly introduced as the boyfriend to the same people a couple of times. Though they were too polite to say.

He knew he had it bad and was probably an even bigger sap than Elias, when thinking about the man made Adam want to seek him out. It had been an hour after all.

"You seen Elias?" He asked Bella as she placed a large bowl of salad on the patio table.

"He was with Bedelia, but I think he may have gone to the bathroom." She replied with a smile. "Missing him?"

"What?" Adam felt his face immediately burn and Bella's smile became charmingly disarming.

"You make a lovely couple. Jack has been singing Elias's praises for months, I think you've been a very positive influence in his life."

Adam returned the smile. "He's been a positive influence in mine."

As he made his way into the house and up the stairs he thought back and couldn't imagine ever believing that someone could have changed his life as significantly as Elias had. Just being there for him, supporting him through anything and everything, accepting him for who he is. Their personalities somehow worked together and Elias remained his closest friend as well as his lover. And of course, fulfilling Adam's sexual appetite was also something he appreciated. When he'd started to transition he didn't think any man would be open minded enough to accept the body he felt comfortable in. Elias had proved him very wrong.

The thought made him stop in his tracks and then take the stairs two at a time as he considered the possibility that Elias may be having some difficulty.

As he got to the bathroom door it opened and he practically fell into Elias. Big arms caught him and then held him once Elias realised who the rude asshole trying to rush into the toilet was.

"Hi." Adam grinned as Elias set him back on his feet but didn't let go.

"Hello." Elias smiled. "We have to stop meeting like this." Elias joked in that wary way he had - unsure if it was actually funny. Adam grinned.

"I was worried, I thought you might be... uh, that there was a situation and maybe we'd need to get home or something." Adam said gently. Whether it resulted in sex or just masturbation, there were times when Elias preferred to be home, and he could imagine this might be one of those moment. Adam had become expert at facilitating Elias's prompt escape to home or somewhere he at least felt more comfortable. It seemed to have had a positive effect on the anxiety Elias often had about his condition.

"No, I'm fine. I needed to urinate." Elias was still smiling and stroked his hand up and down Adam's back. "Thank you."

Adam chuckled. "Oh, like I'm being selfless when I, um… *help out.*" the grin was wiped off his lips by a sudden and deep kiss.

Adam groaned and wrapped himself as much around Elias as he possibly could. They remained like that a long while, in the doorway to the bathroom where they had run into each other sometime before with a very different outcome. They remained like that until Jimmy came to use the bathroom and coughed politely before telling them to get a room.

After another hour of roaming the party completely lost in each other, they'd received enough *aren't they cute* looks from Bev, Jimmy, Bella and even Bedelia, that Adam called time on it. It was early evening and Adam was feeling radiantly in love, he wanted to spend the remains of the day wrapped up in this man as much as he possibly could.

*

"Did you want to have sex?" Elias asked Adam and enjoyed the grin Adam gave him.

"I… damn, you got me good, because actually I just wanted to be alone with you, whether we have sex or not." He chuckled and Elias was warmed by it. Some days Adam was like this. Sometimes because he needed the reassurance and sometimes because he just wanted just to be alone. And alone to Adam these days included Elias. Elias couldn't be prouder or feel more loved by that fact.

Adam closed the front door of his flat and turned to Elias, licking his lips. "But… I'd never say no."

Elias's chest swelled and he thought he might burst from the love and lust that he felt for Adam with every fibre of his being.

"Would you… I think I'd like…" Elias made some hand gestures that had Adam frowning and then laughing before walking over and wrapping his arms around Elias's neck.

"I would absolutely love to fuck you."

Elias felt his cock begin to fill and enjoyed Adam grinding against him. Adam leaned up and kissed him, Elias loved the slide of their tongues. He moved his hand between them and cupped Adam's crotch. He kneaded and palmed Adam's *other* cock, in a way that he knew was at least causing some friction for his lover. Adam's groan into his mouth confirmed it. Then Adam was pulling away and undoing his jeans, he reached in and undid the harness too, letting his jeans and harness fall to the round of his ass. Elias took the invitation and slid his hand beneath underwear and harness, palming at the hardness he found there.

They kissed and touched and made it only as far as the sofa before Elias dragged Adam down to the cushions.

Lips and teeth worked over each other as Elias continued to play with Adam's cock until Adam finally drew back, straddling Elias's hips.

"Stop... I don't want to cum yet, I want to fuck you."

Elias felt heat flush in his cheeks and grunted in response, his own hips jerking up of their own volition.

"Get naked." Adam commanded in that tone that had Elias wincing for fear of cumming there and then. His hand went immediately to his cock in an attempt to calm it whilst Adam got up and went to the bedroom. Elias stood and stripped, stroking his cock a couple of times as he followed Adam.

Adam was stood next to the *sex drawer*. He'd already placed the lube on the bed, and was looking through options, Elias knew. A moment later he turned with a smile and presented the strap-on he had pulled out. Elias grinned in return, it was his favourite, the curve was just right that it teased his prostate in a very very nice way. His cock jerked and leaked precum messily at the thought.

Elias moved to Adam and kissed at his neck as he helped him put on his cock. Adam groaned as Elias's hands wandered, stroking him intimately before the cock was in place, and then up to his chest, splaying hands there in a comforting way that he knew Adam loved.

Adam turned then and pushed Elias down onto the bed. Elias landed next to the lube with a little bounce and Adam was on him, crawling up him until he sat astride his chest.

"Suck it baby." Adam's voice was husky and went straight to Elias's balls.

He opened his mouth and took in the tip of the cock. Adam bit his lower lip as he watched Elias stretch his lips around the shaft. He knew this did something for Adam sometimes, but Elias really preferred to suck Adam's other cock, the pleasure that brought his boyfriend was infinitely more rewarding. Adam watched as he picked up the bottle of lube and poured some onto his fingers, rubbing them together to warm it.

He started to scoot back and Elias chased the receding cock with his lips and tongue, until he wasn't able to move any further forward and it was out of reach.

Adam was between his legs then. Elias raised his hips and put a pillow beneath him as Adam cooed at the sight. Elias's heart swelled. He had no idea before meeting Adam what it could be to be admired in this way. To be so completely loved and supported, condition and all, rather than in spite of it. He knew Adam saw him as a complete package, as he did with Adam. Knowing that Adam loved him - his personality, his humour, and every aspect of his body from his chest hair and penis, to his moustache and his asshole - made Elias feel like the luckiest man in the world.

"I love you." Elias said for the hundredth or maybe two hundredth time that day, as Adam's slicked fingers started to circle his hole.

"Love you too, Elias." Adam returned, a faint smile barely there behind the lust in Adam's eyes.

He was delicate, always so tender with Elias and he had no idea where Adam got the patience. But then his desire to cum was very different from that which Elias experienced. His condition often made him fuck with urgency and cum quickly, but Adam loved him anyway. He even loved when Elias came before he was even inside him, asking Elias to cum on him instead, or if he came on himself Adam would lick it off. The thought made Elias's cock twitch and he started to wonder if he should have put a cock ring on to try and last longer.

He was saved only by the fact that his erection often waned a little when he was first penetrated, as was the case when Adam began to work fingers into him. Perhaps another reason why this was always *so* good!

Elias moaned and writhed as Adam poured lube down the crack of his ass and onto his fingers, slicking them in and out of him and stretching him wider on each pass. The strap-on wasn't too large and Adam knew exactly how to stretch him the right amount for all of their toys.

"You're so fucking beautiful." Adam muttered, his expression glazed with lust that made Elias moan.

"Please Adam, I want you inside me." Elias panted.

Adam nodded and removed his fingers, slicking his cock before repositioning himself. Elias felt the sticky pull against his leg hairs as Adam's lubed hands took hold of him and guided his legs over Adam's shoulders. Elias bit his lower lip and watched as Adam pushed inside him. He wanted to touch himself but knew that would be a bad idea, so instead he gripped the sheets as he groaned.

Adam moved slowly at first, filling him so completely that Elias found it strange that not all men even attempted this at least once, gay or not. That thought was only given more credence as Adam changed his angle slightly and brushed over his prostate. The contact had Elias arching up off the bed and his cock completely hard again.

He writhed and groaned as Adam fucked him, a hazy pleasure on his boyfriend's face. He knew it wasn't the same for Adam, he didn't feel the same sensations as Elias, but he said he enjoyed the way the cock was shaped and ridged inside to make it as pleasurable for him as it could be. Knowing that only served to make Elias all the harder. He loved giving Adam pleasure, and loved just as much when Adam *took* his pleasure, as he was now.

"I'm close…" Elias warned and Adam nodded and panted as he continued to fuck into Elias, getting his prostate on each inward motion until Elias was sweating. He moved his hands to clutch at his curly hair, gripping it to resist touching his cock as Adam pounded him.

The whole bed was moving, the headboard banging against the wall.

"A-Aaaadam…" Elias shuddered as Adam gripped tighter to his thighs and quickened his pace until Elias was shooting hot ropes of cum up his stomach and chest. Elias groaned as Adam continued to fuck into him and he continued to cum. As his cock stopped spurting he reached out and took hold of Adam to stop him. "Too… too sensitive." Elias managed through the orgasmic daze.

Adam nodded and slowed before stopping altogether. He remained, catching his breath for a few minutes before finally pulling out of Elias.

"You didn't-"

"It's ok. I don't always-"

"But I want you to." Elias shifted his legs back down and pulled Adam between them. "I want you to orgasm Adam."

Adam's smile was a little forlorn and Elias knew why. This wasn't the first time something similar had happened. He stroked a hand over Adam's stubbled cheek. He knew as enjoyable as it could be for Adam, he wanted to be able to penetrate Elias with his *own* cock.

Elias huffed and moved, sitting enough to start to undo Adam's harness.

"Elias, what-"

"Shh, I'm going to take care of you." Elias replied, rough with determination as his fingers sought the clasps and worked them open. He pulled the harness away and Adam was panting again. His little cock was hard and Elias had never seen anything more beautiful. He licked his lips and grabbed Adam's hips, guiding him up his body as he went back down, until he lay on his back again with Adam's cock once more teasingly close to his mouth. "I want you to fuck my mouth. You know I love... to... you know I love your cock in my mouth."

Adam groaned, he looked uncertain for a moment but then nodded and shifted so that he was over Elias's face, one hand on the headboard to steady himself.

"If I'm rough just stop me, ok?" Adam asked somewhere between tentative and lustful.

Elias didn't answer, just craned his neck and drew Adam into his mouth, moaning around him and feeling Adam shudder as a result.

Elias slowly lay back and Adam moved forward with him, gripping the headboard with both hands as he thrust slowly a couple of time. Elias used the movements to form his mouth - lips and tongue - into what felt like the best shape for Adam to fuck him. It must have been right because Adam groaned deep and low and then started to fuck his mouth.

Elias grunted and moaned, his hands moving to knead Adam's ass cheeks. He slipped a finger against Adam's back hole, grazing over it and teasing the nerves there. Then pressing at it a little as Adam's hips thrust forward, until with each pull back his finger was almost slipping into Adam.

"Fuck, yes. Oh god, Elias… oh fuck…" Adam's upper body looked beautiful above him, so sleek and wonderfully masculine in the way Adam referred to as *twink-ish*. He still wasn't entirely sure what that meant, but he loved it. Adam was his twink boyfriend, though he'd been told not to introduce him as such.

Adam's thrusts suddenly faltered and he continued a few jerky movements and then groaned, long and deep. Elias felt Adam's cock pulsing in his mouth knew he had cum. His heart swelled at knowing he could give that pleasure to the man he loved.

*

"I'm so glad I met you Elias, even if it was a… a bumpy start."

Adam felt Elias stir, he was likely falling to sleep. Once Elias had been hard again they'd made love, slow and sweet, holding onto each other for dear life as they came together. They were sweaty and messy now but neither cared as Adam curled against Elias's chest, fingers playing in the hair there.

"Yes." Elias's voice was gruff, and Adam smiled, knowing he was holding back a sob. His big softy, wonderful boyfriend.

Adam snuggled tighter to him. "You know, Bev thinks we're going to get married." He chuckled. Then his heart swelled as Elias's breath caught.

"But… we don't even live together yet. Or would we be traditional and not live together until after we are married?" Elias had a tone that suggested he was trying to figure out the logistics, quite seriously.

Adam laughed "I think we are way past anything traditional at this point."

Elias's fingers twitched against him and Adam knew it as an unconscious action - the man wanted to wring his hands together as he often did when nervous or confused, but Adam lay in his way.

Adam propped himself up on his elbow and looked up at Elias. "What is it my big baby bull?"

Elias hesitated to look at him, but then soft eyes met his and a small voice managed "*Can* we live together and get married? Or were you playing?"

Adam went to reply but was immediately cut off when Elias continued -

"No, it's silly. Just Bev being silly and wanting to find more things to gossip about. We haven't been together very long really, and although I love you and of course you love me, people wait longer don't they? We shouldn't rush into anything-"

"Elias!" Adam put a finger to the man's lips before removing it as he leaned in to kiss him softly. "How about we start out with moving in and seeing how things go? Get a place together? You practically live here these days anyway and... well, I don't want to spend time apart when I don't have to." Adam felt a blush rise at the admission so followed it quickly with - "Just because I'd miss your monster cock of course."

"Oh, of course." Elias nodded and grinned, thankfully reading the joke correctly.

Adam moved, straddling Elias and rewarding him with a deep and passionate kiss that had said monster cock stirring beneath him.

Adam had never really believed he would find someone, never ever believed someone would want him - his personality, his body, his baggage. But then he met Elias, and at some point it had become clear, neither of them were alone anymore and never would be again.

ABOUT THE AUTHOR

Max Turner is a transmasculine queer man living in the UK.

Printed in Great Britain
by Amazon